MORE THAN A BODY

MACKINAC ISLAND 2013

MORE THAN
A BODY

For a wonderful, warm summer evening's adventure.

PETER MARABELL

Frances, pour tout

CHAPTER 1

Tommy Marshall is in trouble, and he wants me to help him.

Some people wear trouble like an old glove, but not my brother, Professor Thomas Marshall of the University of Chicago. Trouble for Tommy means returning *Moby Dick* to the library before the fine hits three bucks.

This was different.

"I'm scared, Frank," he said when me called me at home. At 7:00 A.M. He didn't want to talk on the phone, so we agreed to meet at the Melrose Café at 8:30 for breakfast. No time for a run in Lincoln Park. Too bad. It's going to be another hot June day. A morning run is always easier.

I put the telephone back on its cradle, threw back the sheet and sat on the side of the bed. What was Tommy afraid of? His voice was different somehow. Slower, distant. But he woke me out of a sound sleep, so I might be reading him wrong. I pulled on a faded blue t-shirt from the dresser next to the bed. It said "Taste of Chicago" across the front in neon red.

I walked to the kitchen, still groggy. Three scoops of ground Eight O'Clock into the Mr. Coffee machine. Then six cups of water. I headed to the bathroom for a shower. I am the first person Tommy calls with serious trouble. How serious I'll find out soon.

Over the years, Tommy has asked me for plenty of favors, but they were usually no more difficult than tickets for the Blackhawks, or more recently, the Bulls. We'd have dinner, go to a game. I can still get tickets to the Hawks, but when Michael Jordan came to town, Bulls tickets are a tougher nut to crack. I laughed out loud right through the soap and hot water. Tommy was a piece of work. If I told him that I couldn't get him tickets, he often reacted like I was responsible for cutting his personal entitlement program.

Shake it off. This time I had the feeling he was about to ask for a different kind of favor.

I'd just gotten out of the shower when the phone rang again. I let the answering machine get it while I toweled off. It was Ellen. I grabbed my robe and picked up the bedroom phone.

"Hi, Ellen, I'm here."

"Hi, sweetheart," she said. "I was going to leave a message so you wouldn't forget dinner tonight."

"Could I ever forget meeting you, my love?" I offered with a touch of sarcasm.

"Forget, no. Cancel, yes. Are we on?"

"You bet." I said with conviction.

"Okay, see you at Medici at 6:30."

"Ellen." I hesitated. "Tommy called a few minutes ago. I think something's wrong."

"What could possibly go wrong in the History Department?" she asked, adding her own sarcasm. "Gotta go, babe. Tell me later."

I hung up the phone and returned to the bathroom to shave. The partners at Winkler, Norton and Barger liked to see their people bright and shiny every day, although I have room to be different. I am the law firm's investigator. Most of my days are routine. Background checks, digging through county records, but occasionally, it can get unsavory. The attorneys don't care how I dress or what my office hours are as long as they get their information. But every so often I like to fit in. Today, on this early summer morning, I chose a black double-breasted suit, Italian cut, a white shirt and a Guards striped tie. My colleagues will be impressed. Enough coffee. Time to meet Tommy.

I waited for the elevator. And waited. One of these days, I was going to start running the stairs instead of Lincoln Park. All four floors. Think of the time I'd save. Think of the calories I'd burn. When I finally got out the front door, I headed up Oakdale to Broadway. The sun was up far enough up to reach over the rooftops on Chicago's North Side. I looked at my watch. It was 8:40. Tommy was always on time, so I was late.

CHAPTER 2

I walked through the front door of the Melrose Café and spotted Tommy in a booth by the window. He saw me and waved. He slowly lifted his left arm off the table, pulled back the shirt cuff with his right hand and deliberately pointed at his watch. All that was for my benefit, of course. Life is supposed to run on Tommy's terms.

I walked between a couple of empty tables, towards the booth at the window.

"Hello, Frank," Tommy said. "Sit down, sit down. Glad you could make it."

"Hi, Tom," I said as I slid into the seat, reached across the table and we shook hands.

"It's been too long since we, you know, had breakfast."

"Not that long, Tommy," I said. "Couple of weeks ago at the coffee shop in my building."

"Yeah, yeah, but we gotta do this more often," he said, sounding agitated.

Tommy looked like he hadn't slept in days. He looked older, and that was tough for someone who easily passed for a man ten years younger than forty-three. Six feet tall and slender, Tommy still had all his sandy-colored hair, which curled fashionably at the collar of his two-button polo shirt. I bet if I looked under the table, he'd be wearing faded blue jeans and tennis shoes, still the fashion rage for well-groomed college professors. He had changed little, physically, since our years at Michigan State. I was only two years older than my brother, but he looked, well, a lot younger.

Unfortunately, he hadn't moved much beyond adolescence in the emotional department. Especially around women. I introduced him to a colleague at a Hawks game a month ago, and he suddenly began flirting with her, ignoring the woman's husband standing right there. He acted the same way every time he stopped at my office. The receptionist in the lobby, my assistant, even my boss one afternoon. Tommy never understood the difference between a high school dance and a meeting between professionals if there was a woman involved.

Speaking of, I looked around for a waitress with coffee. "You don't look so good, Tommy," I said. "What's going on?"

Tommy looked out the window, not at me. This was going to be a long breakfast.

He turned my way. "How are you, Frank? Things okay?"

"Every thing's fine," I said. Tommy looked out the window again, then back at me.

"How's Ellen?"

"Ellen's fine."

"Good, good. Glad to hear it. When are you two getting married?" he asked, looking out the window again.

"Sometime," I said, "we'll get married sometime."

Tommy looked back at me. He had this dumbfounded expression on his face. "What'd you say?"

"Professor Marshall!" I said, a little too loudly. "Ellen's fine. I'm fine. We'll get married when the spirit moves us. Now where are you? You sure as hell aren't in this restaurant. Talk to me!"

"Don't yell at me!" he said with a hard edge to his voice. "Stop telling me what to do."

"Hey, Tom, you called this meeting, remember?"

His shoulders sagged. "Sorry, Frank. I really am. It's just that..." His voice trailed off for a moment. "It's just that I'm scared. I think my life's in danger."

Finally, we get to it.

"Ah, come on," I said. "Are the boys at the university messing with your promotion again?"

Tommy glared at me, hard. "This is serious, Frank. You didn't believe me when I was a kid. The least you can do is believe me now. All right?"

This wasn't the first time Tommy accused me of not taking him seriously. It started when we were teenagers. We grew up in a quiet, upper-middle class suburb of Detroit. From the outside our life was all "Ozzie and Harriet," but our father, we called him Pop, was a nasty, violent drunk. Tommy and I, more than our mother, were his targets. When I left for college, Pop took it out on Tommy.

"Pop would get so drunk," Tommy said. "He'd start to moan, 'Frank's gone, Frank's gone,' and I knew what was coming. I had no place to hide. You never believed me about Pop."

"Yes, I did. I..." But I let it go. We'd had this discussion before and it never went well. "Come on, Tommy. We're not in Birmingham any more. What's going on?"

The waitress appeared at our table before he could answer. "You gents ready to order?"

"Yeah," Tommy said, and ordered scrambled eggs, wheat toast and hash browns. I ordered pancakes and bacon.

"Thanks," she said. "Be up in a minute."

"Talk to me, Tommy."

Tommy sipped his coffee, "I met a woman..."

"Shit. Not another woman..."

"Stop it, Frank," Tommy said loudly enough that two women at the next table looked over. I smiled at them.

"This time it's different. She's wonderful, and..."

Tommy'd been involved with several women since his divorce ten years ago. Every one of them left him. Apparently he's an interesting companion, but a lousy prospect for the long term.

"Her name's Clare. She's wonderful. We have so much in common."

"But mostly you wanted to jump her bones, right?"

Tommy slowly nodded his head.

"If she's so wonderful, what are you afraid of?"

"Her husband found out. He threatened to kill me. Honest. Said he paid two guys five thousand dollars to kill me. After they cut my penis off." Tommy rubbed his forehead with both hands. "I didn't have any choice," he said. "I had to quit seeing her."

"So?"

"He's after me again. I'm really scared, Frank. You can't run out on me this time." Tommy thought I ran out on him when I left home for Michigan State.

"This isn't Pop we're talking about here," I said. "First, I want to know, are you still seeing this woman?"

The waitress arrived with two white plates filled with our breakfast and more coffee.

"'This woman's named Clare, Frank," he said with irritation in his voice. "It ended six or seven months ago. The affair only lasted a couple of months anyway."

"You're not still involved?"

"No," he said, "I haven't seen her since, oh, I think it was March. Down on Michigan Avenue, shopping."

"But if he threatened you six months ago, and you ended the affair, why are you scared now?"

"Well, last week, she called to say she'd left him for good. He was always angry and hit her too often. She left him and wanted me to know."

"You helping her get away?"

"No. She didn't want any help or anything. She just wanted me to know. Wasn't that nice?"

"Real nice," I said.

Tommy sipped his coffee. "But three days ago, he called again. Her husband, I mean. He said it was my fault that she'd run out on him. Said he's going to kill me. He means it this time, Frank. I know he does. And... and he's got the connections and the money to do it, too."

"Tom," I said, sounding as professional as I could, "some guys say lots of things when they're mad, particularly when the wife takes off, but they don't know who to call for a killing. You can't just call one like a plumber. So who's the husband?"

"It's Rick Morgan, the restaurant guy," Tommy said.

Whoa. My brother had not chosen the nicest people to get involved with. Morgan was as nasty as they come and always traveled with a bodyguard. Rumors had circulated for years about his connections to the mob. Nothing much was proved as far as I knew, but his lawyers were always close at hand.

I'd met Morgan and his wife two years ago when I was looking into something else. Don't remember what, exactly. I didn't like Morgan much. Pushed me around just because I wanted to ask a few questions. One thing's for sure, Tommy's right about Clare Morgan's sex on wheels. A 15-watt bulb, though, as I recall. Maybe she'd smartened up if she'd run out on Morgan.

"Morgan's restaurant supply, actually," I said, clarifying things a bit. "He does have the bucks, that's for sure. The family business is very successful, but the serious money comes from real estate. He owns the apartment building he lives in. On the Gold Coast. Around the corner from the Ambassador East. Not to mention several slum buildings on the South Side." I couldn't help shaking my head at my brother. I didn't mention rumors about the Mafia. Tommy was scared enough already.

"What, exactly, would you like me to do, Tommy?"

"I don't want you to kill him or anything," Tommy said.

"I'm glad to hear that. Geez, you people watch a lot of television. Tom, I dig into people's backgrounds, I don't shoot them. Besides, how's it going to look for a nice college professor to hire a killer?"

"Does that mean you'll help?" he asked with boyish eagerness. "Just talk to him. Tell him I had nothing to do with Clare taking off." He was rushing his words. "Get him to stop threatening me. To leave me alone." Tommy sounded like a kid pleading with his father to make the schoolyard bully go away. It wasn't very appealing.

I picked up the check and looked at the total. "Come on, let's go. Leave the tip."

Tommy dropped two ones on the table and I paid the bill.

It was getting hot fast on the street. I looked for a cab. "Let me see what I can dig up. Then I'll have a talk with Morgan. I'll see if I can convince him that Professor Tom has kept his pants on, okay?"

"Thanks. I knew I could count on you this time."

"Look, Tom," I said, "I'll take care of this for you, but you're through with the wife? I mean, you're clean on this, right?"

"Yes," Tommy said with certainty. "It's finished."

I said goodbye to Professor Marshall and caught a cab for the office.

CHAPTER 3

I got out of the cab across the street from the John Hancock Building. The cabbie handed me change. I handed him a tip. At the newsstand on the corner, I picked up a *Tribune*. The stand was one of those corrugated steel huts reminiscent of the 1940s that still show up on urban streets. The papers lie on boxes in front of the shack and magazines with titles few people have heard of hang in racks on either side of the opening. *Women's Muscles* and *Motorcycle Driver* caught my eye this morning.

Working on North Michigan Avenue was a far cry from my years as a cop. I liked the energy, the feel of the street with men and women dressed for business heading to work. The transition to an office, a real office, with restaurants, bars and shopping only steps away, hadn't taken long.

Sometimes I work late, and when most of the daytime workers are home eating dinner, I'll put on sweats, lace up my Avias and run the four and one-half miles to my apartment. If I want a couple extra miles, I'll head into Lincoln Park on the way. I like to go by the marina, especially in the winter when the docks are up and there's not a boat to be seen.

Winkler, Norton and Barger, P.C. commands a suite of offices on the 15th floor. The firm began 73 years ago when Roland Winkler, grandfather of senior partner, Harold, moved his family from upstate New York to Chicago. "'More crime, more opportunity,' was what the old man always said, and the family's been here ever since," Harold Winkler has told me more times than I can count. The firm's early reputation began in corporate law at a time, the 1920s, when business growth seemed unstoppable. Until the trustbusters changed things, Winkler didn't have to diversify to stay successful, but as the century rolled on, Winkler, then Norton, broadened the base of the firm's legal work. They were masters at spotting trends and taking advantage of the breaks that came their way. By mid-century, Winkler, Norton and Barger was well established, well respected and well heeled.

Despite the contemporary Michigan Ave. surroundings, the firm's suite of offices was a throwback to old man Winkler's conception of what respectable legal offices should look like. Depending on your point of view, the image was either "stodgy" or it was "dependable." The latter is the perspective of three generations of Winklers and two generations of Nortons. As a result, Herman Miller's nowhere in sight. There's not a cubicle nor a movable wall to be found. But oak, leather and thick wool carpeting abound.

The reception area typifies the entire office. Stained oak paneling covers each wall and original paintings, drawings or sketches hang tastefully in carefully selected places. Every chair is a deep brown wood and leather, including the one for the ever-cheerful receptionist, Rose Hall.

"Good morning, Mr. Marshall," she said, reaching under her desk to buzz the security lock. "There are no messages for you today."

I shrugged and headed down a long hallway lined with small offices. Most of them housed our newest attorneys, men and women fresh out of law school, a few with some experience at other firms. My office was at the end of the hallway, on the left. It was a two-office suite, actually, the outer office for Jacque Sherman, my assistant.

"Good morning, Frank," Jacque said in a sarcastic tone, with emphasis on the word, "morning." Jacque's sense of humor is one of her more endearing qualities, but apparently I'm one of the few who appreciate it. She is also tough-minded and clever. Her instincts about people are incredibly accurate. She really ought to be planning legal strategy or helping pick juries. A 31-year old single parent with brown hair and brown eyes, Jacque worked as a staff assistant in the History Department at the University of Chicago for eleven years before I asked her to be my administrative assistant.

"You bet I'll take the job," she said emphatically when I offered it.

"But I haven't told you how much you'll get paid," I said, surprised.

"Whatever it is, I'll take it. This place is a nut house. They're a bunch of dysfunctional neurotics. Except for your brother. Tommy's a nice man. I wonder if you grow more dysfunctional as you accumulate letters after your name?"

My office was no larger than the others, but behind the desk was a huge window, a true indicator of my status. I had positioned my chair so that I could swivel around and look over the tops of lesser buildings to Lake Michigan.

I sifted through the morning's mail. Nothing of interest except the new issue of *Runner's World*. As I thumbed through the magazine, my head was already working on Tommy's problem with Rick Morgan.

Jacque came in and sat down in the chair opposite my desk. I described my talk with my brother.

"That's too bad," she said, shaking her head. "It looks like life after divorce finally caught up with him. You going to help?"

"Well, I can talk to Morgan, I suppose, but I need to know some things first. Call Lt. Kelly, then check our files. See if Morgan pops up anywhere."

When Jacque left, I began looking through my notes. The bottom three drawers of a file cabinet were filled with reporter's notebooks, gathered together by year. Each notebook was three inches wide and six inches long, with a spiral at the top and wide-ruled pages. The odd design allows reporters to hold the book in one hand and write quickly with the other. I always made notes as I worked my cases. Notes on people and places. Sometimes notes on a hunch.

Digging up and keeping track of facts was how I got the job as in-house investigator in the first place. I'd spent a number of years working my way up the ladder from beat cop to patrol car. I didn't like being a cop as much as I thought I would, but I had a reporter's nose for finding out things and the ability to figure out what they meant. I left Oak Park for Chicago's department in the late 70s and met Michael Kelly, then a sergeant. We've been friends ever since. But I needed to change careers, so I enrolled in the University of Chicago Law School at night.

Near the end of my first year, almost twelve years ago now, my answering machine collected a message from Pamela Norton, managing partner at Winkler, Norton and Barger. She wanted to talk about an "employment opportunity," as she put it. I was impressed that Norton made her own calls, so I made an appointment.

On the day of our meeting, Pamela Norton herself impressed me. She was almost six feet tall and in her mid-fifties. Her hair touched her shoulders and could be described as salt-and-pepper. She wore a charcoal, double-breasted suit, a touch of eye shadow and red lipstick that matched the pinstripe in her suit. Her face was narrow, her jaw softly rounded. Her voice was sharp, confident and commanded attention.

"Mr. Marshall," she said, "Winkler, Norton and Barger wants to hire its own investigator."

"Why me?" I asked.

"Because, Lt. Kelly says you're a better fact finder than you are a cop. He also told me you want a change." Norton got out of her chair and came from behind the desk, close to my chair. "Look, we need an investigator. The cops don't have the time and independent PIs can't or won't do the job we want done. Your classes in law school are a plus, as far as we're concerned. Stay in school, don't stay. Your choice. Are you interested?"

It was impossible not to be interested.

We discussed details and then she said, "We did our own check on you. More important, Lt. Kelly says you'd make a tough investigator, and that's good enough for me. Within reason, your methods can be your methods, as long as the information you obtain is the information our attorneys need."

I finished the semester then moved into a real office for the first time. Most of my work for the firm would be to dig up information. My first case, the first of many it turned out, was to run a background check on a prospective client.

Today's case, Tommy Marshall, on the other hand, would be freelance.

Jacque told me that Lt. Kelly was out and would call me back. I spent most of the day rummaging through as many of the notebooks as I could. I also talked to Winkler about two other cases I was working on. I figured I ought to do something for the people paying my salary.

CHAPTER 4

By the time I grabbed a cab to meet Ellen, I hadn't learned anything helpful, but I still had plenty of notebooks left. Rush hour on Michigan Avenue heading north was gridlocked even more than usual. I signaled several times until one cabbie hit his breaks, hit his horn and moved to the curb. I got in and said, "Restaurant Medici." The cabbie cut over a few streets to take North LaSalle. It was a pretty routine ride since he only yelled at other drivers a couple of times.

I got out of the cab on Sheridan, at Surf. It took a few minutes before traffic opened enough so I could do the twenty-yard dash across the street. Restaurant Medici is housed in a converted hotel. When the building went condo, the dining room became Medici. It's a small place if Scoozi is the standard of comparison. Oak booths line a wall and the windows look out on Surf Street. The booths match the hardwood floor and the two-top and four-top tables in the rest of the room. Medici is a quiet, romantic spot for dinner, particularly if you're with someone you love. Plus, it's only a short walk from my apartment.

"Good evening, Frank. Ms. Paxton is already here," the maitre d' said, pointing to a booth at the back of the room.

"Hi, sweetheart," I said to Ellen. "You look smashing for the end of the day." And she did, too. She wore a black turtleneck cotton dress I like very much. It clings ever so nicely to her body.

Her four trips to the gym each week keep her, and her body, looking considerably younger than her 42 years. Gold earrings shaped like flower petals matched her necklace and her light brown hair was pulled back into a short ponytail. I leaned over and kissed her, then sat down.

"Well, thank you very much, my love. It wasn't a bad day, all things considered. A few of my clients even made a buck or two." Ellen Paxton was a vice-president and office manager for a small brokerage house downtown, near the river. She had risen through the ranks to run the office in Chicago, and, so far, had resisted all the tempting offers for promotion to the head office in New York. She loved living in the Windy City as much as I did.

Ellen and I go back five and a half years, when one of her clients, an elderly real estate developer from northern Michigan, transferred all his legal work to our firm. I dug around in the man's life to make sure we had all his bases covered. Ellen and I met for the first time at Medici after work to discuss our mutual client, and the rest, as the cliché goes, is history. It's part of the reason why we have a soft spot in our hearts for the restaurant. It's also a very comfortable place with good fish, salads and pasta.

"Good evening," the waiter said. "In addition to the regular menu, our special tonight is grilled Marlin, with a vegetable and a tossed salad. Would you care for something from the bar while you look at the menu?"

Ellen ordered a glass of Chardonnay. I ordered a martini, with Tanqueray, two olives, on the rocks, very dry.

"Ooh, did you have that kind of day?" Ellen asked, surprised and interested.

"Well..." My voice trailed off, "you know..."

We spent our time talking, as we always do, but I don't remember much of it. I went through two martinis and half of my baked Whitefish Almondine before I realized I was frustrated about Rick Morgan and my brother.

"Some investigator I am," I said.

"What? What did you say?"

"Huh. Oh, nothing. Eat your steak. Want another French fry?" I asked, holding a steak fry in my fingers.

"No," she said sharply. "Something on your mind? It can't be the whitefish you're thinking about, but you keep staring at it." She was right about the whitefish. Maybe I should have ordered the Marlin.

"I'm sorry, honey," I said, sincerely. "I've got Tommy on the brain. He wants me to talk to a guy for him."

"And how is the History professor with the brilliant mind these days?" Ellen asked.

"Well," I said, as the waiter served coffee, "another part of his anatomy has been running around lately getting him into big trouble." I explained the Marshall-Morgan saga as it had developed so far.

Ellen shook her head slowly. "Do you think he'll ever grow up?"

"Who knows."

"You made it, Frank. You got out of that house. You went to school and grew up."

"Yeah," I said, "but Pop really beat on Tommy after I left. Worse than that, Pop convinced him that the beatings were a direct result of me leaving. Tommy believed him. Tommy still thinks I let him down when I went to Michigan State."

"Okay, but that's crazy. You don't buy that, do you?"

"No, but the thing is..." I sipped some water and cleared my throat. "The thing is, I wanted out of the house. I did. I had to get out of there. That's all. It's a damn good thing my parents insisted we both go to college."

"Well, at least they got that right," Ellen said.

"I wish. They would have been embarrassed if we *didn't* go to school. How would they face their friends if Tommy and I stayed home?" Terrible memories, I thought. "I knew Pop would take it out on Tommy if I left. I left anyway."

Ellen reached across the table and put her hand on mine. "It wasn't your fault, Frank."

"Maybe, maybe not," I said. I took a deep breath. "But I have to help him. Tommy came to me. I... I don't want to let him down."

"You can't rewrite the past, Frank."

"I can try," I said, softly.

Ellen sat up and leaned her elbows on the table. "Okay, investigator man," she said, "where do you start?"

"Well, I'm frustrated because I can't remember what the hell I was working on when I ran into the guy who's after Tommy. Name's Rick Morgan."

Ellen took a swallow of coffee and said, "Well, I remember him, dear."

I shot her a startled look. "You! Why do you remember him?"

"The wife," she said. "Blond hair...big chest...small hips... beautiful face. You used to drool every time you talked about her."

"Ellen, that's unfair. Surely I didn't drool *every* time. And, yes, I do remember her. She's got a double-digit IQ and that's giving her the benefit of the doubt."

"I hardly think it was her brainpower that had you on the ropes, sweetie-pie." The "sweetie-pie" slid out of her mouth slowly, with a touch of irritation. "Weren't you freelancing for Lt. Kelly when you bumped into the lovely Mrs. Morgan?"

"That's good, honey," I said. "You're wasting your time selling stock." I thought for a minute. "Let's see...um...Kelly needed some info on a gorilla who worked for the mob and for Morgan. A hit-man, I think."

"Is Morgan in the mob?" she asked. "Is he a member of a family or something?" It was obvious that Ellen's true calling was to be a detective.

"Could be. No proof," I said. "I think Morgan... He's called 'Little' Ricky, by the way, but not to his face...I think Kelly figured Morgan might lead him to the gorilla."

"Well?" Ellen asked.

"Well, nothing," I said. "No information, and all I got for my trouble was a bruised ego. Morgan suckered me with a right hook."

"There's more to it than that, dear," Ellen said with a hefty dose of sarcasm. "You got to meet the one and only Clare Morgan."

I laughed. "She's the reason I got clobbered," I said. "Morgan thought I was more interested in her than the gorilla. Thanks for the memory jog. I'll see what Kelly has to say. Then I'll pay Morgan a visit. I didn't like the way he pushed me. Might be fun to push back."

Ellen stiffened her body at that last crack. She liked me as an investigator. Playing cop or PI didn't sit as well. "I thought you were done with the rough stuff, Frank," she said. "That's what you said, anyway. You've only run into trouble a few times since you left the force."

"Only a couple of times," I said. "I have a pretty sedate life, but every once in a while I run into a guy like Morgan who doesn't take kindly to being told what to do. Anyway, I won't go looking for trouble."

The waiter put the check on the table, between the two of us. Ellen pulled out a credit card and dropped it on the check. "It's on me tonight, my love. Are you going to ask me to spend the night?"

I am, indeed," I answered, smiling.

CHAPTER 5

"**Lt. Kelly called** a few minutes ago," Jacque told me when I arrived at the office the next morning. "My, aren't we a bit causal today," she added, noticing my khakis and a navy Shaker knit sweater covering a black polo shirt.

"No appointments," I said. "Besides, if I'm going to spend the day at the computer and sifting through notebooks, I want to be comfortable."

"Thoughtful excuse," Jacque said sarcastically.

"Smart-ass. While I call Kelly back, see if you can track down Ronnie Birch, okay?"

I met Ronnie when I first came to Chicago. He's part bloodhound, part genius and always a reporter. And he's been on the cop beat for almost forty years, so he knows a lot of people. Anything he could tell me about Morgan would add points to my side. I want to know as much as I can If I'm going to be brazen enough to tell Morgan to lay off Tommy.

Detective Lt. Michael Kelly answered his own phone when I called. "Sorry I couldn't get back to you yesterday, Frank," he said. "You know how it gets sometimes. Jacque tells me you're dickin' around with Rick Morgan. Nothing friendly, I hope." He laughed. "So what's up?"

"Help me out here. I was doing a favor for you when I first got involved with Morgan and his wife, Clare. You remember what you were working on?"

"Jake Stellano," Kelly said, easily. "Soldier for the mob. He'd kill with anything—guns, knives, his hands. Morgan hired him for some reason, probably to snuff somebody."

"Why didn't you ask Morgan yourself? Why did you need me?"

"The prosecutor. Sam Thornton, I think it was. Didn't want us to push Morgan right then. He thought he could finally prove he was connected to the mob if Stellano was ordered to work for Morgan. If Morgan hired Stellano on his own, well, that could have been anything. We hoped Morgan wouldn't notice if you snooped around."

"And was there a connection?" I asked.

"Never found out," Kelly said. "Stellano turned up dead, and that was that."

"Was Stellano set up?" I asked.

"He washed up near Navy Pier with one bullet in the back of the head. What do you think?" he said in a tone that made my question sound silly.

"Was Morgan involved?"

"Never found that out either. Say, Frank, how come you're foolin' around with Morgan?"

"Doing a favor, Mike. Nothing too tough."

"Be careful, my friend. He's a bad man." Kelly hung up without saying good-bye.

I certainly hadn't learned much from Kelly. Nothing that'd help me convince Morgan to leave Tommy alone. At that point, Jacque stuck her head in the door to tell me that Ronnie Birch would meet me at Gray's Place, a watering hole downtown favored by newspaper types.

"Said he'd be there after the last race," Jacque added.

Gray's Place was an old, worn out bar with dingy walls and dingy hamburgers. Ronnie sat on a stool at the far end of the bar, smoking a cigarette. He saw me come in and nodded his head. I took the stool next to him. I ordered a draft. Ronnie must be close to sixty, but he looked haggard, burned out, way past retirement age. He's always looked like that. He wears suits that fit as if he's on a diet.

"How's things, Ronnie," I asked.

"Can't complain," he said, taking a long drag on his cigarette. "Business is good, Frank, real fuckin' good," he added, exhaling, "when the cops are busy, I'm busy."

"Make any money at the track today?"

"Always, Frank," he said. "I always make money at the track." Ronnie rolled the remainder of his cigarette between his thumb and forefinger, then snuffed it out in the ashtray. It wasn't his first, and he pulled another from a half-empty box of Marlboros on the bar. He lit it with a cheap orange plastic lighter.

"You ever going to quit those things, Ronnie?" I asked him. His skin was pale and the neatly trimmed hair on his upper lip was completely gray. Of course, this was a man who worked nights and spent most of his days in the cop house or in bars like this one.

"Did you get me here to bitch about my goddamn cigarettes? Or do you need to get another rich bastard from the suburbs outta jail?" He laughed, then coughed, then laughed again. "You guys call 'em clients, I call 'em dummies. They got money from daddy either way."

I ignored Ronnie's assessment of the firm's clientele and asked, "What can you tell me about Rick Morgan?"

"What would you like to know?"

"The basic stuff, first," I said, "then anything out of the ordinary that might be going on right now."

Ronnie filled me in on the backstory. By the late fifties, just about the time Chicago exploded into "Second City," the restaurant supply business started by his father quadrupled in size. That's when they started buying apartment buildings. Rick Morgan took control of the operation from his father in 1972, when he was thirty-five. It was a friendly transfer of power. His father wanted him to run the business and the relatives all agreed.

But rumors about Morgan and the mob first surfaced ten years before, although nobody ever proved a connection. Now, three decades later, the company he keeps does nothing to quell the rumors. Morgan spends his days with loan sharks, gamblers and pimps but hangs out with the country club set in Lake Forest on the weekends. The cops haul him in from time to time, but his lawyers get him out of trouble as fast as he gets in.

"His suburban neighbors hear the rumors," Ronnie said. "Maybe they get a cheap thrill. You know, like in the movies." Ronnie finished his beer. "Hates to be called, 'little' Ricky, that's for sure."

"Heard that," I said.

Ronnie nodded, "Morgan's one tough guy, Frank. Don't let his size fool you. He always travels with a bodyguard."

"Heard that, too," I said. "What about his personal life? Anything I ought to know?"

"Clare," he said, savoring the name. He signaled for another beer. "Jesus, Frank, what a broad. Ever meet her?"

I nodded.

"Damn, I'd give anything to spend a night playin' hide the salom' with her. Broad's got to be forty if she's a day. But what a body."

Ronnie lit another cigarette. He looked like he needed it. He waxed on and on. I finally interrupted. "Uh, Ronnie, I don't mean to break into your fantasy world, but can you tell me if anything is going on with Morgan and his wife?" Ronnie looked like he was coming out of a coma.

"Nothing for sure, Frank, but I hear things. Let me make a few phone calls. See what I can turn up. I'll meet you here tomorrow night, same time."

"Okay," I said. "Beer's on me." I put a five and a one on the bar and said good night.

CHAPTER 6

The next morning, Jacque informed me her computer search had come up empty. "Morgan's name didn't show up at all. Not even in connection with our clients whose activities are, shall we say, questionable."

I sifted through the mail and made a couple of calls. I had a mid-morning meeting with Phyllis Barger, the third name on the front door. I needed to report on a case given to me by her protégé, a young attorney from Yale. Pretty routine, but my mind wasn't on it.

When I returned to my office, Jacque had gone to lunch, so I settled in with another stack of reporter's notebooks. My notes fell into three categories: facts, analysis of those facts and, finally, my hunches about anything related to the people and the events.

Six phone calls, one fax and a tuna salad sandwich later, deep in the eighteenth notebook, I found what I was looking for.

The first few pages focused on Jake Stellano, not on Morgan. The information came straight from Lt. Kelly. Stellano was second-generation in this country, and his life in the mob was pretty clear. He'd spent his first thirty-three years in Chicago. He was running messages on the West Side before he got to junior high. Stellano killed his first man at seventeen. He used a clothesline to strangle a gambler who owed a lot of money.

He had an alibi, of course, but the cops never believed that he'd spent the whole evening eleven miles away helping two aunts move furniture.

In this case, the cops suspected that Morgan had hired Stellano to kill somebody, and that would have required mob approval. Make the connection, and Morgan could be tied to the mob. Never happened. They never made the case.

My notes read: "Talk with Jake—then Morgan." But that never happened either, because Stellano never left Morgan's side. He even slept in a wing of Morgan's Lake Shore Drive apartment.

After following them around for ten days, I decided to look Morgan up at his office. The sign over the door read: "Morgan Imports."

He had talked to me, "out of curiosity," I'd written. "He bought my story, I think." I don't remember what nonsense I concocted to cover why I was asking questions. Then the notebook read: "Nothing worth telling Kelly."

In the next entry, I said: "Talk to CM alone"—that meant Clare—and "Where do they hang out?" I remember Ronnie Birch had told me they spent a lot of time at the Pump Room in the Ambassador East Hotel. It was around the corner from their apartment. My note read: "Thursdays... Pump Room. Good man, Earl." That was Earl Jaworski, the bartender. He reminded me of Sasha, the bartender in Rick's Café in "Casablanca."

The whole Pump Room scene looked like a set from an old movie. Lots of leather and wood. So-called quiet elegance. When Earl pointed out Clare to me, it was all I could do not to gawk like a high school kid. She must have been five-seven or five-eight, and her blond just-off-the-shoulder hair and white skin were in marked contrast to a tight, floor-length black sheath dress. It was slit up the right side to mid-thigh. The neckline scooped into a couple of folds that showed her ample cleavage. When she sat down in the booth, under Arlene Dahl's picture, I walked up and introduced myself.

For the next few minutes, Clare Morgan did two noticeable things. She flirted with me in a way that can only be described, as I wrote later in a notebook, "hot." She also kept one eye focused on the door behind me. Suddenly, her banter and body language, particularly her repeated efforts to let me see her breasts if I was so inclined, and I was, abruptly changed. So abruptly, in fact, that I turned around. Morgan and Stellano walked straight at me. Just as I was about to say hello, Morgan's right hand came out of his jacket pocket and hit me square in the jaw, and down I went. He must have had something in his hand to hit that hard. Probably a roll of dimes.

Morgan leaned over and warned me that Clare was off limits. If I ever got within ten feet of her again, he said, he'd kill me. Stellano grabbed me by the ankles and dragged me between the tables out onto the street. There's your "quiet elegance" for you.

I didn't end up learning anything to help Lt. Kelly with his case, but I wrote some interesting comments about Clare including, "the sexiest woman on two feet." I closed the notebook. Guess I'd better not show that one to Ellen.

Ronnie Birch sat on the same bar stool as the night before. "On me tonight, Frank," he said, raising his glass in my direction.

"Okay by me." I ordered a draft. We sat in silence until I'd emptied half my glass.

"Only thing worth talkin' about is the broad," Ronnie said finally, and laid out vivid details about an affair between Clare and "some guy," as he put it. "Morgan's got tapes of 'em. Video tapes."

"Video tapes!"

"Yeah. Tapes of them fuckin' and other things. Burned up the screen, that's what my guy told me. Burned up the screen."

"How the hell'd he make tapes?"

"Beats me. Can you believe that shit?"

"But how could he do it? Takes a lot of set-up. Lots of time."

"I don't know, Frank. But all the tapes are in the same hotel room."

"The same room?" I asked. More and more surprises.

Ronnie nodded his head.

"Did you find out who she was screwing?" I was pretty sure I knew the answer.

"You're not gonna like it, Frank," Ronnie said. "It's your brother. It's Tommy. Can you believe that?" He started to laugh, but caught himself. "What the hell did Clare Morgan see in a stuffed-shirt professor? I mean, it doesn't take a fuckin' genius to guess he wanted a piece of her ass. Hell, I want a piece of her

0

ass, but I ain't gonna piss Morgan off. I don't care how good she is. Not me. No way."

"Is the affair over?" I asked.

"Seems so," he said. Ronnie also told me that Clare skipped town, and that Morgan was more than a little angry. He hasn't found her despite his connections.

"One thing bothers me, Frank," Ronnie said. "Broad's gotta have help. No way she can hide from Morgan without help." An ugly thought about Tommy popped into my mind.

I had to ask. "Got any ideas who might do that?"

"Nope," he said.

I swallowed the last of my beer and got off the stool. "Thanks, Ronnie." I said. "I owe you one."

"Not for the beer," he said, "not for the beer."

I was turning to leave when Ronnie said, "Frank, I'm sorry about your brother. Tommy's got a real problem if Morgan's after him."

I nodded and headed for the door.

CHAPTER 7

It was after nine by the time I got to Ellen's apartment. She lived two blocks from my place on Chicago's North Side, a comfortable, safe and pleasant part of the city. The five-block area around Clark and Broadway offers a variety of mom-and-pop stores. Lindeman's Market has fresh vegetables, cheeses and a deli while Jacobson's is an old-fashioned drug store with a lunch counter. Owner Len Jacobson's only concession to the 1990s is the most extensive video rental selection in the neighborhood. Lincoln Park, in the other direction, towards Lake Michigan, is like a huge four-season backyard with trails, picnic tables and a zoo.

Ellen's apartment, befitting her status and income, is pretty upscale compared with mine. The building has only four large apartments on two floors and each living room faces the street. Ellen's place has two bedrooms, a remodeled kitchen, hardwood floors and plenty of storage. She likes American antiques and oriental rugs, with a few carefully chosen watercolors and photographs. It was elegant without being pretentious.

I hung my jacket over a chair in the kitchen, slipped off my shoes and settled into a big overstuffed chair next to the couch where Ellen sat reading *The Nick Adams Stories*. Last week it was *The Sun Also Rises*.

"Hemingway, again? Are you reconnecting with your northern Michigan roots?" I asked.

"No. It's not just Hemingway. I've been reading Fitzgerald, Steinbeck and Faulkner, too. They're really good. And fun. I haven't read them since I was in school. Now I understand why all those teachers insisted we had to read certain books."

"It isn't that you're more attracted to macho bullfighters the older you get?"

"Not as long as I can indulge my half-baked fantasies with you, my dear," she said. "Speaking of half-baked, how about some food?" We both groaned at Ellen's humor, then got up and went to the kitchen.

While I heated the sauce and watched the pasta cook, I gave Ellen a rundown on what I'd learned. I needed Ellen's help sorting out the details, and I wanted her two-cents worth, too. She made a tossed salad and we drank a cheap Cabernet while I talked.

"You really think Tommy's through with Clare Morgan?" Ellen asked finally, picking up silverware and napkins.

"Hell, I don't know," I said, and poured more wine into my glass. "I honestly don't know."

I dished up two generous portions of penne, spooned Marinara sauce over the pasta and handed one of the bowls to Ellen. We went into the living room and ate quietly at the coffee table for a few minutes.

"What would you do, my love," I asked, "if you were me?"

"Talk to Tommy again. That's the first thing. You have to find out if he's still involved with Clare." Ellen sipped some wine and added, "If he's not done with her like he told you...well, if I were in your shoes, I'd be pissed."

"Uh, huh," I said. "I'm pissed just thinking about it. I don't like the notion that my brother would be stupid enough to get involved with Clare again, or that he might have lied to me."

We picked up the dishes from the table, rinsed them under the tap and loaded the dishwasher. Being the observant fellow that I am, I noticed that Ellen had become uncharacteristically quiet.

"What's up, kiddo?"

"Well, I'm trying to figure out why a mild-mannered college professor would get involved with a mobster's wife."

"Great sex with a gorgeous woman comes to mind," I said. "And we don't know for sure that Rick Morgan is a mobster."

"But, Frank, since his divorce, Tommy's hung out with a lot of women, all of whom, according to him, want to screw his eyes out." Ellen paused for a moment, then said, "Maybe I ought to rephrase the question. Maybe it should be 'why is Clare Morgan involved with a mild-mannered college professor like Tommy?' After all, she's got plenty of money, likely other lovers. Why him?"

"Good question, my love," I said, "good question. Perhaps the professor's the good sex partner."

"For crissake, Frank, your brother's in trouble. Can't you think about anything but sex?"

"Not when you look as sexy as you do right now," I said. I was perfectly serious.

"Sexy? Sexy!" she said, looking down at her clothes. "I'm wearing faded jeans and a sweatshirt with paint stains all over it."

"I know," I said slowly, "I know." I put my arms around Ellen's waist and pulled her to me. She returned the favor by putting her arms around my neck and pressing hard against me. We kissed. "Think I'll spend the night," I said.

"I sure as hell hope so.

"Walk this way, sweetheart," she said, tugging gently at the belt buckle of my pants.

I followed.

Later, as we lay in bed, lights out, stereo off, Ellen said, "Are you going to call Tommy?"

"We don't have to talk about it right now." She rolled onto her side, put her head on my chest. I put my arm around her shoulder.

"We do have to talk about it. If you can't let go of the idea that you owe Tommy because of the past..."

"I'm not that hung up on the past."

"Yes, you are," Ellen said. "You think you've got to get Tommy out of this jam to let yourself off the hook for what happened a long time ago. You have to let go of the guilt. You gotta do this, babe."

"Okay, okay. I'll call him first thing in the morning."

Ellen sat up in bed and pulled the sheet up around her waist. Her breasts were silhouetted against the light filtering through the window blinds. "Frank," she said, "if Clare Morgan doesn't need Tommy for sex, and it certainly isn't for a professor's salary...then...why does she need him?"

CHAPTER 8

I had an appointment with Denise Kirshner, a close friend of Harold Winkler's. She was more interesting than most of the firm's clients, and her company, DCN Manufacturing, was an important part of the firm's business.

I scanned her brief to get up to speed. Until the age of forty-two, Denise's singular accomplishment in life had been to marry Tyler W. Kirshner when she was seventeen years old. He was thirty-four. For the next twenty-five years, she travelled everywhere in the world, sightseeing, while Tyler entertained himself with an unending string of beautiful young women who were always seventeen or eighteen years old. Denise knew of his escapades, of course, and wasn't above retaliating by spending more of his millions than she might otherwise have done.

But as so often happens in stories like this, Tyler died of a massive heart attack and Denise's life changed dramatically.

That was as far as I'd gotten when Jacque stuck her head in the door.

"The secretary in the History Department said Tommy's in class 'till after lunch. She'll have him call ASAP."

"Thanks," I said. I pushed Kirshner's file aside and picked up the notebooks containing what little I knew about Rick Morgan. Maybe going over them again would help. I was reasonably sure that his rumored mob connection offered nothing useful for confronting Morgan. Going through the notes another time only convinced me of that.

A call from Lt. Kelly gave me a piece of information worth knowing, however. Morgan had a new bodyguard. A guy named Tony Vanelli.

"He's tough," Kelly said, "he'd kill you without thinking twice, but only if Morgan gives the order. He'd never act on his own. Vanelli used to work for Gotti in New York, and he's got a thick file. Been arrested for just about everything from car theft to murder, but he's only done a few years for assault. Just thought you'd like to know."

Jacque walked in the door. "Rose just called from the lobby. There's a woman here to see you."

"I don't have any appointments until Denise Kirshner this afternoon, do I?"

"She doesn't have an appointment, Frank, but you'll want to see her."

"Oh, and why is that?"

"Because her name is Clare Morgan," Jacque said with a grin on her face.

"No kidding! Well, send her in." My heart, while not skipping a beat necessarily, began thumping away at a pretty good clip. For once, I was happy that I'd worn a suit. Too bad it wasn't more stylish.

"Mr. Marshall," Jacque said in her a-client-is-here-to-see-you voice, "this is Clare Morgan."

And indeed, it was. Her tall, slender body stood in the doorway. She wore a navy suit and carried a small, matching leather attaché case. The skirt fit well and stopped three inches above the knee. The jacket had two vertical rows of large round brass buttons like a military tunic. Her blond hair was parted on the right side and brushed back behind her ears. Even with a suit on, it was easy to tell that Clare was in spectacular shape. If her body was that of a forty-year old, as Ronnie Birch seemed to think, there wasn't a twenty-year old woman I knew who wouldn't trade her for it.

"I'm sorry for barging in without an appointment," she said, "but I thought you might have a few moments to talk."

"I'd be happy to spare a few moments, Ms. Morgan," I said. Of course, I was thinking more in terms of the rest of my life on a desert island. "Please sit down."

Clare settled in the leather chair across from my desk, put the attaché case on the floor next to the chair and carefully readjusted the skirt in her lap so it would rest another inch up her thigh. She hadn't needed to do that. The skirt was revealing enough leg without additional help.

"Mr. Marshall, I'll get right to the point," she began.

I'd hoped for an invitation to join her in lusty activities, or at the very least, a proposal of marriage.

"I saw Tom last night, and he told me that you were going to talk to my husband and explain that Tom and I are no longer involved. Is that correct?"

If ever there was a verbal equivalent of a cold shower, the words, "I-spoke-with-Tom-last-night" were it.

"I thought you'd already left the city," I said.

"No, not yet. I've been staying with friends in Wrigleyville. My husband knows where I am, unfortunately. But he wouldn't dare send his goons to get me. Now, Mr. Marshall, are you going to talk with Rick?"

"I told Tommy that I'd probably talk with your husband," I said, emphasizing the word, "probably."

Clare explained that her affair with Tommy lasted only a few weeks. She'd been extremely vulnerable when she first met him because she had just learned that her husband was sleeping around. But the affair with Tommy was over, and she felt the whole thing was her fault. She was very sorry that her husband had threatened Tommy.

"I imagine," she said, "that except for some of the details, you already know most of the story. Therefore, I suspect you're wondering why I came to see you."

Maybe the always gorgeous, always sexy Clare Morgan wasn't so dumb after all. I decided not to say anything, and see what would happen.

After a long, uncomfortable silence, she said, "Mr. Marshall, what I'm about to tell you could mean trouble for all of us... you, me, Tom, so I hope you would think carefully before you tell anyone else." She cleared her throat. "Mr. Marshall," she said, "I'm leaving my husband, I'm leaving the country, and you and Tom are the only two people who know. I've almost got the details worked out. It'll take, oh, two, perhaps three weeks for everything to be ready."

"And then?"

"And then I'll vanish. And since you're probably wondering, I'm going alone. No one, not even Tom, will know where I'm going or precisely when I'm leaving. I want it that way. Now, here's what I'd like from you..."

Clare Morgan was getting smarter by the minute.

"I'd like you to talk with my husband, as you already plan to do," she said. "Right now the sonovabitch is watching me like a hawk. Every move I make. As long as he thinks I'm involved with Tom, I can't get out of the country."

"Don't you think your husband will wonder why you dropped in to see me?" I asked.

"I shop at Water Tower all the time," she said. "I slipped out the back, where they drive the cars through. I'll go back in the same way. My husband's got a very sheepish man following me today, so I've spent a lot of time with bras and panties. The guy's too embarrassed to get close. He'll never know."

Cool and meticulous were new words I added to my description of Clare Morgan.

"If you can convince my husband," she continued, "that Tom and I are through, he'll ease up on me. I know he will. That will give me the room I need. I am prepared to pay you for your services, of course." With that, Clare reached over the side of the chair, and picked up the attaché case. She put it in her lap ,and opened the lid so only she could see inside. When her hand came out of the case, she placed a small stack of bills with a red rubber band around it on the desk in front of me.

"One-hundred thousand dollars, Mr. Marshall, in thousand dollar bills. It's yours as long as you promise that you will see my husband in person and convince him that I am no longer having an affair with your brother."

"Well," I said, clearing my throat, "that's certainly a lot of money, but I won't promise to do something that may not be the best way to handle the problem."

"I thought you said…" She seemed flustered for the first time since walking into my office, but she quickly regained her composure. She reached into the case and pulled out another stack of bills that matched the first.

"Two hundred thousand, Mr. Marshall," she said with an edge in her voice that told me she was not often turned down. "I'm quite certain that two hundred thousand dollars, in cash, I might add, is considerably more than your annual salary."

"The first stack is considerably more than my annual salary," I said. I wondered why Clare was willing to pay so much money to hire me to do something that I was going to do anyway. Could it be just a coincidence that she and Tommy wanted me to do the same thing? I picked up both stacks of bills, fanned them once just for the hell of it and handed them to Clare.

"Look, Ms. Morgan, how about this," I said. "I'll talk your husband, but as a favor for my brother, not as a job for you. Besides, it's not worth that much money. And just so there's no misunderstanding, I have no interest in spoiling your plans to leave the country. I'll keep that piece of information to myself." I stood up and extended my hand across the desk. "I wish you well in your life without your husband."

Ms. Morgan stood up, dropped the money into her attaché case and closed the lid. She shook my hand, turned and left without saying another word. It was obvious that Clare Morgan usually got her way.

CHAPTER 9

The fog was beginning to lift off the lake by the time Tommy returned my call. I didn't mention Clare's visit. I wanted to see his reaction when I told him about it, so I invited him to have dinner with Ellen and me at my apartment. I also wanted Ellen's take on the affair. She'd convinced me that there was more to this saga than either Tommy or Clare were telling.

I filled Ellen in while we drank some Chenin Blanc, tore into a loaf of French bread and waited for my brother. She listened quietly until I got to the part about Clare Morgan's unannounced visit.

"Wait a minute," she said sharply. "Do you think the professor put her up to this? More important, did you drool?"

"I don't know if it was his idea, or if he sent her. Maybe we can figure that out when we talk to him." I also explained that house rules at Winkler, Norton and Barger prohibit drooling in the office.

Ellen didn't dignify my attempt at humor with a response, but said, "You don't trust Tommy on this, do you?"

"Well, I certainly don't trust Ms. Morgan. And I've got this uneasy feeling about my brother." I poured each of us another glass of wine. "You know, I don't trust him, either, even though it makes no sense for them to still be involved. At the very least, Morgan will keep the pressure on both of them."

"Yeah," Ellen said, " but since when did common sense get in the way of hot sex?"

"Whoa, hold on there," I said, "now look who's dragging sex into the conversation."

When Tommy arrived, Ellen uncorked another bottle of Chenin Blanc while I put a small roasting chicken in the oven. It had been quite a while since Tommy and Ellen talked, so we sat in the living room while the two of them caught up. She told him about the offers to go to the home office in New York, and Tommy described the latest goings on in the "ivory tower." I nibbled on bread and sipped my wine more than I talked, since I'd heard most of this before. But I picked up in Tommy's voice, in his manner of speaking, that eight-year old child I'd seen from time to time. The one who whined more than he described his life. He sounded like all his entitlements to the good life had been stolen from him by the big-bad academics-turned-bureaucrats who, of course, had it in for him from the start.

As we sat down at the table to eat roast chicken with red skins and asparagus, I made my move. "Clare Morgan stopped by the office to see me today," I said.

"No kidding?" Tommy responded. "How about that." His attempt at surprise had a hollow ring to it, but I was pretty sure he was lying when he deflected my comment by changing the topic. "Is she one helluva good-looking woman, or what, Frank?"

"She is, indeed, an attractive woman," I said, meeting eyes with Ellen.

"You know," Tommy said, looking wide-eyed first at me, then at Ellen, "Clare's really a wonderful woman. Oh, I know that most men take one look at her and only think about screwing her, but behind that blond hair and dynamite body is a woman who..." His unsolicited adoration continued unabated for almost five minutes. When he wasn't extolling her virtues, he entertained us with some of their merrier adventures.

"Then you didn't have any idea that the lovely Ms. Morgan was going to see Frank?" Ellen interjected when she had listened long enough. Her tolerance for discussing Clare Morgan was at an all-time low.

"I did not," Tommy said, emphatically. "I told her Frank was going to talk to her husband about us. I didn't even say that much until she told me he was watching her all the time." He looked at me now. "I guess I thought it might make her feel better if she knew you were going to help me, Frank. And it should help her, too. Right?" He looked at both of us for some kind of response. "Right?"

"I just want to make sure I've got this straight, Tommy," I said. "Was it your idea that Clare come see me?"

He shook his head.

"And you didn't know that Clare came to the office today?"

He shook his head again.

"All right, Tom, whatever, but I want to ask you one more time, are you through with her?"

"Just how many times do I have to tell you, Frank? Huh? How many?" There was an edge to his voice. He wasn't angry, he was hurt. "I'm not seeing her anymore. Is that clear? We're done. Now what are you trying to do?" He was almost shouting. It felt like we were teenagers, at home, a long time ago.

"Look, Tom," I said. Now I was the one who was angry. "You want me to ruffle the feathers of a nasty guy who's convinced he's got you and the Mrs. pegged. If I'm going to do that, I want to be damn sure I know the whole story. If I give him my word that you're not screwing his wife any more, I want to be telling the truth. Do you understand?"

I couldn't tell if he understood me or not. He was headed in a different direction.

"You guys just don't know what it's like," he said, "you really don't." He leaned forward, his elbows on the table, palms of his hands turned up, and a soliloquy began…

"All my life, I've always done what other people told me to do, goddammit. Always! First, it was that father of ours. 'Cut the grass. Trim the walk. Wash the car.' I did all that shit, but it was never good enough. Never! And that's when he was sober. He'd start swinging if he was drunk. He never did that to you, Frank. Never to you. Always telling me what to do. Oh, and women. Ha! Women! He never liked one goddamned woman I dated. Did you know that, Frank. Did you? Not even my wife. Drunk or sober, he said my wife wasn't good enough for me. Oh, and as long as I've brought up my wife: Christ, every time she opened her mouth, she slammed me for something. 'You drink too much, just like your father,' she'd yell. All the fucking time, 'you drink too much.' All I wanted was one lousy martini after work. Is that too much to ask? I never got drunk. I never hit anybody like Pop hit us. I'll tell you a thing or two about my wife. Frigid. Cold. That's what she was. Cold! Said… said I was a rotten lover. Took her eleven fucking years to tell me I was a rotten lover. Who gives a shit? You can ask Clare how good I am. She'll tell you."

I'm not sure who Tommy was talking to, but it didn't feel like us.

"And then there's the President and the Dean. Fuck 'em both. 'Publish or perish, publish or perish.' If I hear that line one more time, I'm gonna shoot the fuckers. And Rick Morgan. Who's Rick Morgan, anyway? He doesn't give a shit about Clare. She's just a trophy to him. The sexiest woman in the city goes home with Morgan every night. With Morgan! Shit! Do you know who gave him the nickname, 'Little Ricky?' She did, that's who. You know why? Well, I'll tell you. Little Ricky. Get it? 'Little?' Every guy's got a hard-on for her but Morgan. He can't get it up, but Little Ricky takes her home. Well, I want to take her home with me. With me, do you hear me? With me! I'm the one she loves. Not him. But no. I can't have her. Morgan says I can't have her. You say I can't have her. Why the fuck not? Huh? Will somebody tell me why I can't have the best thing that's ever happened to me?" Tommy's breathing was rapid, labored, as if he'd just run a couple of miles but was out of shape.

The adolescent had returned, full force. I ignored the child and pretended I was dealing with an adult man. "Are you still having an affair with her, Tommy?"

He hesitated. Was he trying to calm down or think up an answer? "No, Frank, I'm not involved with Clare any longer."

Tommy declined Ellen's offer of coffee, explaining that he had an early meeting with students at the office. After he left, we cleared the table, poured some coffee and sat on the couch in the living room.

"I don't really know what to say, Frank," Ellen said, reaching for my hand. "It's a side of Tommy I've never seen before. Have you?"

"In small doses, nothing like this. I've seen spoiled children act that way when Santa Claus doesn't come through, but this..."

"Frank, we're not talking about kids or Christmas here. You're brother's a professional, a college professor, a man others look up to, especially his students. I don't know who that was, but it scares me to think that he teaches in a classroom." Ellen shook her head.

"Do you think he's telling the truth?" I asked. "Could he fake a performance like that?"

"I don't think so"

"So does that mean you trust him?"

"I guess so," she said. "Do you?"

"What choice do I have? Clare says the affair is over and offers to put two hundred grand where her mouth is. Tommy says it's over and demonstrates his disappointment with a spectacular tantrum. You make it a complete sweep because you don't think he could fake the performance." I threw up my hands.

Ellen went to the kitchen. She poured more coffee for both of us, emptying the carafe. "So you'll see Morgan, then?" she asked.

"I don't know any other way. I can't trust him, but I can't let him down again, either. I just can't."

"I know," Ellen said, softly, "I know."

"I'll go to Morgan's office tomorrow. Try to make it simple and business-like."

"Are you going to take your gun?" Ellen didn't liked the idea that I could get hurt. Over the years, I'd seldom been roughed up. In fact, Morgan was the last guy to do that. It'd been a long time since I carried a gun, although as an investigator, I've got a carry permit. I kept the gun at the office, in the bottom left drawer of my desk. It was always clean and well oiled.

I shrugged my shoulders. "Maybe I should. Especially since Morgan's got a new bodyguard." I drank the last of my coffee. "And I'll bet he hasn't forgotten that he sucker-punched me the last time we met."

"What bothers me," she said slowly, "is that you haven't forgotten the sucker-punch." Ellen put her cup down on the coffee table and wrapped both arms around my neck. "I do worry about you sometimes, my love."

"I know you do, sweetheart, I know you do. I'll be careful. I have no particular desire to mix it up with Morgan or his sidekick."

"Yeah, but you wouldn't pass up an opportunity to get even."

CHAPTER 10

My eyes snapped open. It was six-twenty. I was ten minutes ahead of the alarm clock. Low adrenalin was already pumping. Adrenalin keeps me on edge when I need to be.

I'd set the alarm early, so I'd have enough time for a long run in Lincoln Park. I needed to think through how I would approach Morgan. No interruptions, no unwanted suggestions, just me and the problem while I ran.

I pulled navy running shorts and an oversized T-shirt from the dresser next to the bed. The shirt said, "Chicago Marathon 1992" across the front. I'd been a course worker not a runner.

I was anxious to get out, but it was nervous energy not an overeager desire to exercise. I put coffee and water into the Mr. Coffee machine before I left. After almost an hour in the park, I'd decided how the day ought to go.

First, I'd just show up at Morgan's office. That would signal that I respected him as a man and a businessman. I didn't, of course, but if being deferential would catch him off guard, I was for it. Then, I'd simply tell him about Tom and Clare and explain why it was in his best interest to believe me. If that didn't work …well, that's as far as the plan went.

I took a shower and shaved. I called for a cab while I dressed: a solid black suit and a white shirt—for power—and a wide-striped tie.

At the office, Jacque handed me the mail and a small stack of messages. I quickly leafed through both, but everything could wait. I opened the left-hand bottom drawer of the desk and took out a Smith and Wesson .38 with a two inch barrel and a brown leather hip holster. A box of shells and a cleaning kit shared the drawer. I checked the gun, opened the cylinder and spun it. It was empty, of course. I closed the cylinder and pulled the trigger. Clack! I loaded the .38, but put it back in the drawer.

I was not going to take the gun.

No good looking for trouble.

I told Jacque where I was headed and why.

"You think this is the best way to handle it?"

I nodded my head.

"I know you well enough to trust that you've thought it through, but I'm worried that something could go wrong."

"He's my brother, Jacque. I'm only going to talk to Morgan. I can't think of any other way to handle it."

"Be careful, Frank. I'd hate to have to work at the university again."

I caught a cab in front of the building and gave the driver the address.

Morgan Imports, the company founded by Morgan's father, had moved to an empty warehouse on the West Side in 1985. The warehouse took up most of a city block. Although the serious money was in real estate, Morgan Imports was a thriving company with a reputation for good service and fair prices. Lt. Kelly explained to me that a successful business provided a better cover for Morgan's mob activity than an unsuccessful one.

I told the cabbie to stop at the corner near a small glass door. The hand-painted sign that read "Morgan Imports" was a much smaller version of the one perched above the freight entrance in the middle of the block. The office entrance was obviously newer than the rest of the building.

I paid the cabbie and got out. I adjusted my suit jacket, walked up to the door and went in as if I had an appointment. The office was a medium-sized room. No partitions, counters or pictures on the walls. Three olive green desks with tan Formica tops formed a T-shape in the middle. A row of similarly colored file cabinets lined the back wall. Women occupied two of the desks. The third had no chair and was covered with small file boxes.

The woman at the desk nearest the front door was probably forty-five with black hair cut close and oversized bifocals with burgundy rims. She wore a white cotton blouse buttoned up to the neck. The other woman was in her twenties, but her baby face made her look even younger, like a high school cheerleader. The red bow attached to her ponytail didn't help.

"May I help you?" Ms. Bifocals said.

"Yes," I said, smiling, "I'd like to see Rick Morgan."

"Do you have an appointment?" She didn't bother to look down at the open book on the desk. She already knew the answer.

"No. I don't have an appointment, but I hope you might be able to squeeze me in. I just need a few minutes." If she was the gatekeeper, maybe acknowledgement of her authority would help. "My name is Frank Marshall."

She got up and walked through a door at the back of the room. I heard voices on the other side, then footsteps and the door opened. In walked Rick Morgan, Ms. Bifocals, and a huge man I took to be Tony Vanelli, the new bodyguard. Morgan was five-five or five-six. He looked to be fifty-five, and what was left of his black hair was combed straight back. He wore a gray silk sharkskin suit, a black shirt and black tie. Trendy. He was pretty thick in the middle, and the suit jacket tugged at the buttons in front.

Ms. Bifocals went back to her desk. Tony Vanelli stepped forward and said, "What-a you want?" Vanelli had to be six-six and three hundred pounds. He must have played football somewhere along the line, but he was soft now. His face was dark and puffy, and the few steps he took told me he wasn't particularly quick. He wore a navy cotton jacket over a black T-shirt and the awkward bulge under his left arm told me where his gun was.

I ignored Vanelli and his question. "Mr. Morgan, I'd like to talk to you for a few minutes. In private."

"About what?" Morgan asked.

"About Professor Thomas Marshall."

Morgan's body stiffened. "You got nothin' to say to me, smart guy."

"Yes, I do," I said, "and I think you'll want to hear it."

"Fuck you. Tony, throw the sonovabitch out."

Vanelli stepped in front of Morgan, no doubt protecting him from whatever might happen next.

I took one step forward and said, "Morgan…"

But I never finished the sentence. Tony drew his gun with his right hand and pointed it at me. It was a .45 automatic. As much for show as anything, he deliberately reached up with his left hand and slid a round into the chamber. "Out."

The two women watched Morgan leave the room. Ms. Bifocals sat calmly. She'd obviously been through this stunt before, but the cheerleader looked as if she was going to throw up.

"Okay, Tony, no trouble. I'm on my way out." I slowly stepped backwards towards the door. "Would you mind calling me a cab?" I said with a straight face. A thin smile broke on Ms. Bifocals' face, but Tony was not amused. He moved in my direction.

"Out," he said again.

Well, so much for planning. I'm not sure why I thought the business approach would work. Maybe I wanted it to work, so there'd be no trouble. But I guess that if I want Morgan to listen to me, there will be trouble. I'll remember that next time.

It took a few minutes of fast walking before I found a cab. Back at the office, I called Ellen. "How about a late lunch, sweetheart. I've got a few things I'd like to run by you."

"Sounds like fun. Someplace fancy, I hope?"

"Actually, what I had in mind was you picking up some antipasto salads and bread at Dominic's and we eat here. I want Jacque in on the discussion."

"Do I take that to mean that you've already talked to Morgan and it didn't go well?"

"Not well at all."

"You okay?"

"I'm fine, but it's time to shift to plan B."

"What is plan B?"

"I don't have a plan B," I said. "That's why I suggested lunch."

Shortly after 1:30, Ellen arrived at the office carrying a large brown paper bag. Its contents filled the air with wonderful smells, but, then, I was hungry. Ellen and Jacque chatted while I got a yellow legal pad and some pencils. This wasn't the first time the three of us had brainstormed a case. Three minds were, indeed, better than one. Ellen and Jacque's instincts about people added a dimension I needed.

"Why don't we use the small conference room," I said, pointing down the hall. We sat down in the leather chairs surrounding the round oak table and opened the Styrofoam containers, spreading out the salads, bread and white plastic utensils. Between mouthfuls, I explained what happened at Morgan Imports.

"So where do I go from here?" I asked. "What are my alternatives, and which one has the best chance to work?"

"I have a question I'd like to ask first, Frank," Jacque said. "Is this really necessary? I know how you feel about your brother, but will it do any good to talk to Morgan on Dr. Marshall's behalf?"

It was the right question, one I'd asked myself. I also knew the answer.

"It is necessary, Jacque," I said. "I owe my brother... a lot. Besides, he's not used to dealing with guys like Morgan or Tony Vanelli."

"And you are," Ellen said. It was a statement, not a question.

"Yes," I said, "I am."

We spent the better part of the next two hours eating and talking. When the salads were gone, Jacque got us coffee and a large plate of fruit, both of which were plentiful in the small kitchen across from the conference room.

"Let's see what we've got so far." I shuffled several pages torn from the legal pad. Each one was half-full of writing. "Okay, I'll see Morgan again, and tell him Tommy and Clare are done. We assume that talking to Morgan means dealing with Vanelli. And that probably means a fight. A fight with Morgan is less likely, but a possibility. Since we assume there'll be trouble, wouldn't I be better off picking the time and place to meet Morgan?"

"It won't be a meeting, Frank," Ellen said. "He'd never do that after what he did this morning." Ellen picked several red grapes off the plate. "You'll have to catch him in a place he won't expect to see you."

"Good point, Ellen," Jacque said. "How 'bout a public place? Somewhere open, somewhere it'd be hard for Morgan to start any rough stuff. Too many witnesses."

I thought for a minute. "The Pump Room," I said, "in the Ambassador East. That's where Morgan used to hang out all the time. It'd be easy enough to find out if he still does."

I went back to my office and grabbed my address book out of the center desk drawer. Sure enough, there was Earl Jaworski's number. Earl had been the head bartender at the Pump Room for ages.

I rang him up and he answered the phone. I explained what I wanted.

"Every Tuesday, Thursday and Saturday," Earl said. "Just like clockwork. Yep. Just like clockwork, Morgan and that sexy broad of his. About 7.30, give or take, they'll come in and sit in the booth in the corner, under Arlene Dahl."

Back in the conference room, the three of us talked about the Pump Room and a rapidly shortening list of alternatives.

"Well," Ellen said, "it seems to me that the Pump Room is the best place."

Jacque nodded her head and so did I.

"It's public, dignified and there are bound to be enough people to provide more witnesses than Morgan wants to worry about."

"And, I can pick the night," I said. "No matter when I show up, the surprise will be on my side. Morgan won't easily be able to throw me out." I swallowed the last of the coffee. "I'll take my gun this time. In case one of them does something stupid."

CHAPTER 11

I picked Tuesday for my surprise visit.

About 8:30, I clipped the holster to my belt, went downstairs and hailed a cab in front of the Hancock building. By the time I got to the Ambassador-East, I figured Rick Morgan and Tony Vanelli would have had a couple of drinks. With no alcohol and plenty of adrenalin pumping, I ought to have the edge.

Shortly before nine I walked into the hotel lobby, turned left and went into the Pump Room, one of the most well known of Chicago's watering holes. Like the offices of Winkler, Norton and Barger, the Pump Room was a world of leather and wood. It always impresses, even if it's out of date.

"Hi, Earl."

"Hey! Hey, Frank. Long time no see. You still snooping for the stuffed shirts on Michigan Avenue?"

"You bet. Beats working for a living. How's the Mrs.?"

"Swell, Frank, just swell. We're heading to Disney World next week. Don't that sound great?"

"Sure does, Earl." I looked over at the booth under the picture of Arlene Dahl. Tony Vanelli sat there alone. "Say, Earl, I see Rick Morgan's pal baby sittin' Arlene." I nodded my head towards the booth. "Is the master around?"

"Un, huh," Earl said, "at the hors d'oeuvres table." He pointed towards the far wall. "Over there."

Sure enough, there was Morgan with a full plate of food in each hand, walking back to his booth. A few steps behind him, carrying only one plate, was Clare Morgan. I looked back at Earl. "Where the hell does he get those pants with the little ducks on 'em anyway?" The pants were apple green, the ducks were small and tan. He wore a matching tan polo shirt and a camel blazer. Must be his after hours uniform.

"Beats me, Frank, but look at her. Geez." Every man in the room was looking at her. Blond hair brushed back behind the ears like the other day in my office, very tight navy leather pants, a matching scoop necked top, more than enough cleavage. And gold. Gold around her slim neck, on her chest between her breasts, on her wrists, on her toes for all I know.

"Back in a minute," I said to Earl. "Think I'll have a chat with our friend."

"Careful, Frank. If Morgan's hands go into his pockets, the right one comes out wrapped around a roll of dimes."

"Un, huh," I said, rubbing my chin, "I've met the dimes before."

I was still ten feet away from Arlene's booth when Vanelli saw me. He whispered something to Morgan. Morgan and Clare looked up, at me. Morgan nodded his head in my direction and Vanelli put his napkin on the table and got up.

"Sit down," I said in an easy tone, "sit down. I just want to talk to your boss." I glanced at Morgan.

"You talka my boss, I breaka you face."

"Christ. What do you do besides wet-nurse Little Ricky here, write bumper stickers?" I saw a very thin smile on Clare's face, but I knew calling him "Little Ricky" would piss him off. It did. Vanelli moved my way, but Morgan's left hand shot out and caught his sleeve.

"It's okay, Tony, Marshall's just leaving," Morgan said. He looked at me with an icy glare. "Go on," he said, "get outta here, asshole. Never call me that again. Capisce?"

"Got it," I said, "but listen, about Tommy Marshall. He's not such a bad…"

"Fuck 'em," Morgan said, "he's dirt."

"Yeah, well, he was messed up a while back. You know how college professors are." Clare's mouth barely cracked another smile.

"Fuck 'em."

"You already said that. Look, Morgan," I said, "Marshall will stay away from you, from the Mrs., from trouble. That's not too much to ask is it? He's all through with Clare, she's not going to leave you, so why not forget it?" Morgan looked as if he'd been stuck with a knife when I mentioned Clare leaving.

"Shut up, dick head," he said, angrily. "Shut up or I'll take care of you just like I'm going to take care of…" He stopped in mid-sentence, but I knew the finish. It was time to push harder.

"Little Ricky," I said, knowing it would ramp up his anger, "I'm only going to tell you this once, so pay attention. Leave Tom Marshall alone or I'll make it my business to see that you leave him alone. He's my brother. This is personal. Capisce?"

With that Morgan came out of his seat. "He's mine, Tony."

I spread my feet even with my shoulders, my weight balanced. Vanelli hadn't moved. Morgan was in front of me now. I watched his hands. He wasn't going to sucker-punch me a second time.

"You're a punk, Marshall." Morgan spit the words at me and stepped close enough to strike. His hands slid into his coat pockets.

NOW! My left arm began its upward arc, palm of the hand flat, fingers pulled back. My arm accelerated.

Before Morgan's hands could move, the stiffened palm of my left hand caught him at the base of the nose—CRACK!—and kept right on moving at the same velocity for two more inches.

"Aaaah!" Morgan hit the floor like a sack of potatoes.

Clare hadn't moved an inch and neither had our audience of patrons, but Vanelli was now only a step away. He reached under his jacket, but my right arm moved faster. The barrel of my .38 rested comfortably against Vanelli's jaw, just in front of his ear.

"Go ahead, tough guy," I said, "pull the gun."

He froze.

"Good thinking, Tony. Now take the gun out of the holster, with the other hand, like a good boy and drop it on the floor."

He did. I kicked the gun backwards, well out of reach.

Morgan sat on the floor and the only thing to come out of his pocket was a handkerchief for a broken and bloody nose. Tony wasn't moving, and neither was anyone else in the place. I put the .38 back into its holster at the small of my back. I bent over the still-seated Rick Morgan.

"Morgan," I said, "I've got a deal for you. I'll keep my brother far away from you and the Mrs. and you stay far away from him. Remember, this is personal. Capisce?"

Morgan nodded his head. That was good enough for me.

I stood up and straightened my coat and tie. I noticed that Clare had no smile on her face. That seemed odd considering that Morgan had just given her escape plans a green light. I backed up five steps just in case Tony decided to do something foolish. He didn't. I turned and walked towards the door.

"Good moves, my man," Earl said, "good moves. The cops are on the way. I'll have to give them your name, you know."

"It's okay, Earl," I said. "Tell Lt. Kelly to call me."

When I hit the fresh air, I took a deep breath and headed up the street.

All in all, it had gone pretty well. I'd done my good deed for the day. Trouble was... I wasn't sure if the good deed was helping Tommy Marshall or putting Rick Morgan on the floor.

I'd just opened a beer when someone hit the outside buzzer. It was Lt. Kelly.

"Come on in, Mike. You remember Ellen, don't you?"

"Of course I do. How are you Miss?" He tipped his hat in her direction. "It's been some time."

"Yes, it has," she said, extending her hand. Kelly wasn't sure what to do, but he awkwardly reached out.

"How are you, Mike?" she asked.

"Fine, Miss. Just fine. I'd be a whole lot better if our friend here hadn't caused such a ruckus at the Pump Room," he said, pointing his thumb, hitchhiker style, at me.

"Come on, Mike," I said. "I thought you'd be happy I messed up one of the bad guys, for crissake."

All three of us were standing at the door. Ellen turned sharply and went into the living room. Mike and I followed.

"Frank, I don't care if you work Morgan over," he said, "but in the Pump Room? You shouldda picked the cop house steps. Save me the trouble of coming over here. Two guys from the Mayor's office watched the whole thing. Didn't know that, I don't suppose. Why, they were all over me when I got there... 'can't have a drink in peace, guys fighting,' they said." He shook his head. "Say, I could use a beer, if you don't mind. I'm off the clock."

I got up and passed Kelly a bottle of Beck's from the refrigerator. Ellen hadn't said a word. She sat on the couch, arms folded, a grim look on her face. I started to say something, but Mike put up his hand and I stopped.

"The least you coulda done was wait for us to get there. Those Mayor guys had a field day when they found out I knew you. Accused me of, what's the phrase." Mike thought for a moment. "Oh, I remember now, 'coddling criminals.' Yep, that's what I do, 'coddle criminals.'"

"What'd you say?" I asked.

"Nothing. Not a thing. I just nodded my head and did my job. I've run into political types before. Always keep my mouth shut and do my job."

I ran through the details of what happened for Mike, but it was obvious that Ellen wasn't getting any less angry as she listened to my tale.

When I got to the part about leaving, Mike interrupted, "Arrogant, Frank, that's what you are, arrogant. You break up a peaceful night at the quietest bar in town, and what do you do? You walk out. Why'd you walk out, Frank? Will you tell me that?"

"More dramatic," I said. "Makes Morgan and Vanelli think I'm tougher than I really am."

"Speaking of tough, the bartender, what's his name? Jaworski? Says you put Morgan down quick and clean. Where'd you learn that chop-chop stuff anyway?"

"College," I said, "I told…"

"That's enough!" Ellen said. "I've heard enough." She was standing now. "You're all alike." She gestured at Kelly. "You don't care what Frank did. You don't care that he started a fight. You only care where he did it because it caused you a problem." She looked at me now. "You're proud of yourself, aren't you? Sucker-punched the bad guy. Finally got even, didn't you, Frank?" Ellen walked into the kitchen and said no more.

Kelly stood up, finishing his beer. "Well, I best be on my way. In my office at nine o'clock tomorrow morning, Frank. Understand?"

"I'll be there."

Good night, Miss," Kelly nodded, but Ellen only gestured a good-bye.

"Ellen," I said, but she cut me off.

"You don't get it, do you? You pick a fight in a restaurant to settle a score? And Mike thinks you did a good job?

"I know you worry about me getting hurt..."

"That's not the point. Yes, I worry about you, nasty people are a part of your job sometimes. I know that. This is about *what* you did, Frank. How are you different from the bad guys if you pull shit like that?" Ellen leaned on the kitchen counter and glared at me. "Sometimes you just piss me off."

I started to say something, but Ellen said, "Not now."

CHAPTER 12

I run faster and longer when the summer heat gives way to cool, dry days of late fall. My legs have more spring, and fewer runners crowd Lincoln Park. Could be, too, that life was easier with Tommy out of trouble. In fact, I hadn't talked with him since I got Morgan off his back.

I'd been less successful with Lt. Kelly and his boss, Capt. Pat Dickerson. They rode me pretty hard, but when Morgan refused to file assault charges, and the manager at the Ambassador-East didn't want any bad publicity, that was that. My work at Winkler, Norton and Barger returned to background checks, trips to the courthouse and routine appointments.

But not today. Harold Winkler had made an appointment with me for Denise Kirshner. According to Harold, all was not well in DCN Manufacturing's boardroom. I scanned the file, trying to remember what I'd read and when. It appeared that the problem began when Denise's philandering husband died of a heart attack, and Denise suddenly became the majority stockholder of a company she knew nothing about. That did not sit well with her stepsons, Tyler, Jr. and Kyle, who'd expected to become president and CEO, respectively. Stepdaughter Elizabeth, however, held just enough stock to announce during an emergency meeting of the board that she was willing to give her stepmother one year to prove she could run the company.

And Denise Kirshner did just that. At fifty-two, she'd run DCN Manufacturing for ten years. She'd turned out to be a quick learn. Sales, profits and dividends were all up, much to the consternation of her stepsons.

But that focus on her new career hit the skids six months ago when she met Jason Donaldson, a twenty-eight year old high school graduate who worked on the DCN loading dock. First, she presented him with a company award for efficiency. Then, the two took up together and Jason moved his blond-haired, blue-eyed 6-foot frame into Denise's bed and into her office as her executive assistant.

The stepsons hit the roof. They asked Winkler, who asked me, to investigate the handsome Mr. Donaldson. Gentle pleadings from Winkler had done little to convince Denise to dump him. With the investigation complete, it was my turn to try.

Denise Kirshner sat in my office looking every bit the CEO in a soft gray Anne Klein suit and a rose silk blouse with a large Hermés scarf tied at the neck. She looked younger than her fifty-two years, much younger. Her black hair was cut short, to the top of the ears, and brushed back on the sides. She obviously spent time keeping her body in shape.

"Mr. Marshall, let me be clear. I'm only here because Harold Winkler asked me," she said.

"Ms. Kirshner," I said without much conviction, "I'm sure Mr. Winkler has your best interests at heart." But Denise Kirshner seemed quite capable of taking care of herself. "And so do your children, I'm sure," I added. She shifted uncomfortably in her chair.

"Winkler, yes," she said, "but Kyle and Tyler only want the business. I'm afraid that Elizabeth is about to give it to them since she doesn't like my romance any better than her brothers. So why don't you tell me what I already know and get it over with."

I told her what I knew about Jason Donaldson. Pretty boy, airhead and gigolo cover the bases. She was not impressed.

"All right, Mr. Marshall," she said, "I listened to you. Now it's your turn to listen to me. I know about Jason because I ran a check on him five months ago. He'll ditch me one of these days, but in the mean time I'm having a ball. My husband was a jerk, to put it mildly. He fucked more teenage girls than I can count. And he threw it in my face. Well, Jason makes me feel like a woman. He wants to make love to me every day and I love it. Is that clear?"

I nodded my head.

"I pay all the bills. I pick up all the tabs. I can afford it. I control the money and Jason'll never get a penny more than I hand him. I want to play with this man for as long as he'll play back. When he leaves, I'll chalk it up to experience, or some damn thing, and maybe find another young hunk who's dumb enough to believe that lots of sex will get him lots of money. Then again, maybe not. Now, I have..." The telephone rang twice, so I knew it was Jacque.

"Excuse me," I said, and picked up the phone.

"Frank, you're not going to believe this, but Tom Marshall and Clare Morgan are in the lobby. They want to see you right away. Supposedly an emergency."

"Take them to the small conference room." I put down the phone and looked up at Denise Kirshner. "I'm sorry for the interruption. It's an unexpected crisis."

"Most of them are," she said sarcastically, "most of them are." She looked at the gold Rolex on her left wrist. "Mr. Marshall, in thirty seconds, I'm going to Harold's office and have him draw up papers to transfer half of my company stock to my stepdaughter. What she does with it is her business. I'll be protected because the rest of my stock, and twenty-percent of the before-tax profits each year, will go to a numbered Swiss account belonging to me. I already have a few dollars there. The day after tomorrow, Jason and I fly to Paris, then to the south of France for a cruise on the Mediterranean."

With that, Denise Kirshner stood, shook my hand and said good-bye. Jacque came in as Denise left. My mind spun to my surprise visitors.

"In the conference room?" I asked.

"Yes. Neither one said a word."

We walked down the hall and entered the room together. Tommy and Clare were sitting at one end of the oak table, next to each other, holding hands. Not a good sign.

I closed the door. Jacque and I took seats across the table from them.

"We want to talk to you alone, Mr. Marshall," Clare said, nodding in Jacque's direction. She was all business.

"Ms. Sherman stays. Period." I wasn't in a mood to be nice. "Now what the hell is going on, Tommy?"

"Frank," Tommy started to say, but Clare touched his arm and he stopped in mid-sentence. It was clear who was in charge.

"Mr. Marshall, I love Tommy. We are leaving the country tonight. Together. Where we're going is our business. We'll be safe from my husband and we'll have enough money to live a comfortable life."

I looked over at Jacque, but she was staring out the window.

"Tommy," I said, ignoring Clare, "What the fuck is happening here? I don't see you for what, three, four months. Then you walk into my office ready to run off with Clare Morgan in the middle of the night. Are you nuts?"

"Mr. Marshall," Clare said aggressively, before Tommy could answer. "We didn't come here to give you our itinerary or to get your approval. We came here to warn you because you're Tom's brother. He loves you. It doesn't take a genius to figure out that my husband will be very angry at you for convincing him that we were no longer involved."

Tommy turned his head slowly to the right and looked at Clare, moonstruck, like a high school sophomore.

"So this was all a set up?" Jacque interjected, waving her arm in the air. "To get your husband to quit watching you? To give you more time to get away? Is that what it was? You didn't worry very much about Frank's safety last summer."

Clare did not respond to Jacque, but looked at me. "Tom was sincere when he came to you," she said. "He thought our romance was over. But it was never over for me. Once my husband quit having me followed, well, I went to Tom. I told him that we could get away if we planned carefully enough. That my husband wouldn't find us it we did it right."

Jacque shook her head. "Why should we believe anything you say? Will you tell me that, Ms. Morgan?"

I didn't wait for Clare's answer. "Tommy, is this what you want? Are you crazy enough to get involved with the Morgans again? He's going to find you, you know."

"Mr. Marshall," Clare started to say, but she'd spoken for Tommy once too often.

"Shut up," I said hard, and slammed my fist on the table. "Talk to me, Tom. I want to hear it from you."

This time Clare let him talk.

"What d'ya want me to say, Frank?" He was agitated, upset. "Huh? What? That I love Clare like... like I never thought love could be? Is that what you want to hear from me? Is it? Huh?" The all too familiar eight year-old child was back.

"Tom, just help me understand why you'd do such a damn fool thing."

"Because I love her and she loves me. That's why. Clare wants me, Frank. You heard her. She loves me. Nothing else matters. Just us. Everybody I know has love. But not me. Well, I'm just as good as you, Frank. Just as good as all of 'em. I'm, I'm... bright and... and funny and a great lover. Isn't that right, honey? It's my turn to have the love I want. Do you hear me, Frank? Do ya?" Clare never took her eyes off me while she gently stroked the back of Tommy's head, almost playing with his hair. It was very unseemly.

"Yeah, Tom," I said, letting out a deep breath, "I hear you."

"So where will you go to keep Morgan from finding you?" Jacque asked.

Clare lightly touched the side of her right temple and smiled, like she was dealing with a group of twelve-year olds. "As I said a moment ago, our itinerary is none of your business. When my husband comes calling on you, Mr. Marshall, I don't want to worry that you'll tell him where we are."

"Oh, Clare," Tommy said, shaking his head, "Frank'd never do anything like that."

"I'm sure he wouldn't, dear," she said. The "dear" had a distinctly condescending air about it. "But some men behave unpredictably with the barrel of a .38 stuck in their ear." The dumb blond routine no doubt gave Clare an edge. She was tough.

"And now it's time we end this pleasant conversation, we have much to do." Clare was already out of her chair and halfway to the door before Tommy caught up with her. "Don't bother," she said over her shoulder, "we can find our way." Clare closed the door behind them.

Jacque and I sat for a couple of minutes without saying a word.

"Well?" she said.

"Well, what? What can you say about a dumb-ass move like that?"

"For one thing, I can't believe that any woman who looks like that, is as crafty as she seems to be, would find that whiney behavior appealing. I'm sorry to say that about your brother, Frank. That's not the Professor Marshall I know."

"Unfortunately, I have seen that side of him before. More times than I like to think about. What else?"

"Well, perhaps the lovely Ms. Morgan has another agenda. One that doesn't include Dr. Marshall."

"You think she planned all this?" I asked. "Starting last year when she met Tommy and had the affair?"

"I don't know, but I wouldn't be surprised."

"Me, either," I admitted, "but it's going to take some doing to hide from Rick Morgan."

We talked for a while longer, then Jacque said, "Frank, do you think she's right that Morgan'll want to get back at you for lying to him?"

"Probably," I said, nodding my head, "probably."

CHAPTER 13

By 4:30, I'd finished three reports, filled Winkler in on my meeting with Denise Kirshner and missed lunch. I had two hours before meeting Ellen for dinner at Medici, so I pulled a tan leather duffel that held my running gear out of the closet. If I got a move on, I'd have enough time to run through the park on the way home. I needed time to think, time to clear the cobwebs out of my head about this whole matter. A lot of questions didn't have answers. A lot of behavior didn't have motives.

Getting out of the building in running clothes is a hilarious task. The people in my office hardly notice anymore, although some of the women whistled and laughed. Riding the elevator to street level is another story. I might as well have an Easter Bunny suit on for all the stares.

One hour and ten minutes later, I stood in the shower with the hot water pounding on my head. My body thanked me for the exercise, but none of the fog around Morgan, Clare or Tommy had cleared. Did Clare plan the whole thing, as Jacque suggested, or did she take advantage of the situation to get away from her husband? Or both?

I toweled off, brushed my hair and decided that I didn't need to shave again. I put on a pair of khakis, a navy polo shirt and a heavy ecru cotton crew-neck sweater. I laced my Avia running shoes back on and walked the two blocks to Medici.

"What difference does it make if Clare planned it or not?" Ellen said after I told her about my visitors. I ordered a carafe of house wine, a dry white. Ellen ordered Greek chicken, I wanted scrod. We split a Caesar salad.

"It just does, that's all," I said. "If she's ruthless enough to plan something like this... I don't know... it just seems pretty callous."

"I think you're splitting hairs, sweetheart. Besides you said yourself that getting away from Morgan was almost impossible. Maybe the only way to do that is to be ruthless and single-minded."

"Do I detect some defensiveness on your part? Are you sticking up for your gender?"

"What if I am? Clare Morgan deserves a good life just like any other woman. Is it her tactics that bother you?"

The waiter mixed the salad at our booth, dished up two large plates and left them on the table with slices of French bread.

"Maybe Clare is doing what she has to do given who she's dealing with," Ellen said. "After all, extreme measures for the average housewife might be normal for a Mafia woman."

"Ellen, we're not sure Morgan's in the Mafia. It's not fair to say that."

"Now's who's being defensive? Why the hell are you sticking up for a scumbag like Morgan? On a good day, he ought to be shoved in front of a bus." Ellen picked up her wine glass, took a deep breath and followed it with a swallow of wine. "Look, Frank, I think you're having trouble with the idea that Clare Morgan is more than a body with blond hair. You sized her up wrong. She's very good at creating a façade because she has to be. Maybe you're finding it hard to accept that a woman can be that tough."

We were interrupted when the waiter brought our entrees.

"Ellen, you were mad the other night because I picked a fight in a public place, and now you're suggesting that I can't handle smart, aggressive women. Like I got a testosterone problem?"

"I'm just saying. That's all."

"Well," I said, cutting into my scrod, "let me think about that for a while, okay?"

"Of course," she said. "Anyway, there are a few other questions that occur to me."

"Such as?"

"Such as, why is Clare hanging with Tommy in the first place? And why are they being so thoughtful about warning you? And why are they being so public about leaving the country? They could leave separately and meet up later."

I thought about that. "The obvious answers are that Clare really does love Tommy and they... Tom anyway... didn't want his brother to get surprised by Morgan. Trouble is, I'm not sure I believe either one of them."

"What about leaving together, publicly?"

"No answer for that one, my love," I said. "If she's as clever as you seem to think, that's a dumb move. Unless..."

"Unless she wants it known that they're together."

"I just had the same horrible thought," I said. "She wants Morgan to know that she and Tom are leaving together. That we

84

all lied to him. In fact, she's going to make sure he does know. Christ, he'll go off like a rocket."

"Yes, maybe it's all a diversion to give her more time. Morgan's pissed at you, he's pissed at Tom. First he goes after you to beat back the humiliation. Then he goes after Tom and Clare."

"We shouldn't have to wait too long to find out if we're right."

The waiter was back again. "Could I interest you in dessert? Dutch apple pie or a raspberry parfait?"

Split a piece of pie?" Ellen asked.

I nodded.

"And black coffee for two, please," she said. "You staying with me tonight?" I asked. "I've been thinking about your skin next to mine for the last twenty minutes."

"Actually," she said, lifting her cup to her lips, "I have been thinking about a few body parts myself."

"No kidding. Anything you'd like to share with the man on the other side of the booth who's quite turned on by your very presence?"

Ellen sipped her coffee thoughtfully. "How about joining me in the shower for a big hug and kiss?"

CHAPTER 14

When the telephone rings in the middle of the night, it is unexpected, disorienting, alarming. I'm annoyed if it's a wrong number, but I get back to sleep. If the caller's actually looking for me, on the other hand, it's never happy news.

I groped for the phone, moving only my arm. It must have rung four or five times, if ringing is what electronic telephones do these days. I finally found the receiver and said hello.

"Frank Marshall?"

"Yeah. Who's this?" I tried to sound awake.

"Ronnie...it's Ronnie Birch, Frank," the voice said. I hadn't talked with Ronnie since last summer when he gave me the information on Rick Morgan.

"Ronnie!" I said. "What the hell d'you want? What time is it anyway?"

"Four, four-thirty, I guess."

"What d'ya want, for crissake?" I felt Ellen move beside me.

"There's trouble, Frank," Ronnie said. He sounded unhappier than I did.

"What kind of trouble?" Ellen was awake now. She put her arm on my shoulder.

"It's your brother, Frank."

Ronnie had my attention now. I sat up on the bed. "Come on, Ronnie, don't play games."

"Rick Morgan's got him, Frank. He's pissed. Said he's gonna cut his fuckin' nuts off 'cuz he fooled around with his old lady."

"Jesus. Where are they?" Ellen was sitting up now, too. She turned on the lamp beside the bed.

"Couple of blocks from here," he said. "I can take you there."

"Where the hell are you?" I said.

"The zoo, man. I'll meet you at the north gate of the zoo."

"In the park?" I said.

"Yeah, in the fuckin' park, man," he said. "Where d'ya think? In the fuckin' lake?"

"Be there in twenty." I hung up the phone and told Ellen what Ronnie had told me while pulling on jeans, a T-shirt and socks.

"I'm scared, Frank," she said. "It's the middle of the night. Anything could happen."

"I'm not happy about it either. But if Morgan's got Tommy, I've got to help him." I put on a sweatshirt and an old pair of running shoes. The clothes were all dark colors. I grabbed my Detroit Tigers cap and put it on backwards.

"Why don't you call the cops?" Ellen asked.

"And tell them what? Meet a guy at the zoo. He'll take you to a bad guy who's holding my brother hostage? In the middle of the night?"

"Listen Frank, I don't like guns, but maybe this time you should take yours."

"It's at the office. Can't take time to get it now."

Ellen put on my big white terrycloth robe and leaned against the bedroom door. She looked beautiful.

"See you," I said. "I love you."

I didn't wait for the elevator. I took the stairs to the basement parking garage and found my car gathering dust at the end of the third row. I seldom use it in the city, so it sits for months at a time. My friendly Ford dealer assured me that a Taurus sedan could handle the idle time without protest. It started on the first try and I pulled slowly out onto Oakdale. It wasn't particularly cold for the middle of October, but a light mist quickly coated the windshield. I turned on the wipers and pulled the washer lever.

I took Sheridan Road south. The trip took far less time than the twenty minutes I told Ronnie. I wanted to get there first. Near the bottom of Lincoln Park, I parked at the first fire hydrant and grabbed a small black nylon bag from under the driver's seat. It unfolded into a single layer rain jacket. I walked into the park. I didn't see anyone, not on the sidewalk, not in the park. No druggies, no gangs. Maybe the streets were safer.

I could see the gate at the north end. It was closed and, presumably, locked. I'd check it if I had to. No one in sight. My instincts are saying something is wrong. Meeting Ronnie may not be all that easy.

About fifty feet from the gate was a large elm tree. The ground under the tree was damp, but not wet, so I sat down and watched the gate.

I looked at my watch. Ronnie was fifteen minutes late. I didn't like it. I thought about going to Morgan Imports, but Tommy wouldn't be there. Too obvious. I could call Tommy or Ronnie, or both.

Five minutes more and I'm outta here, I thought. The longer I stay, the better the odds that I'll get caught in something.

Time to go. I looked as far as I could into the mist. I didn't see anyone in the park or near the gate. I got up, brushed off the seat of my pants and walked slowly, quietly out of the park. No one followed.

I caught the edge of a blur as I reached for my keys. At the car, damnit! I should have expected it. They wouldn't come at me when I was watching for it.

I tried to duck, but his shoulder was lower than mine. He hit me full force in the chest and stood me straight up, slamming me backwards against the side of the Taurus. I couldn't breathe... couldn't get air. I slid slowly down the side of the car and sat on the pavement, holding my stomach, waiting for the pain to pass. I focused my eyes just enough to see three pairs of shoes in front of me.

I put my hands flat on the pavement and tried to push myself off the ground. It didn't work. I heard a voice say, "Stand him up."

Giant hands I assumed were attached to some of the shoes grabbed me under the arms and hoisted me up. Tony Vanelli and another very large man I didn't know, held me securely. Their arms were locked around my arms, and my hands were pinned at my sides. Giving the orders was Rick Morgan. I had a nasty feeling this wasn't going to be fun.

"Hi, there, fuck," he said. "How ya doin?"

I didn't have enough wind to say anything.

"Aw, what's a matter? Cat got your tongue?" Morgan laughed, and so did the other two. He opened his jacket, pulled out a long, thin cigar and lit it. He drew in heavily and blew the smoke in my face. "Maybe that'll help," he said and laughed again.

It didn't help.

"I suppose you're wondering why we asked you to this little gathering," he said. "Well, I want to discuss a few things with you. Like honor, trust and being good to your word. Shit like that. Know what I mean?"

"Where's Tom Marshall?" I said with as much air as I had.

"The good doctor?" Morgan said. "Your brother who was so messed up? Is that who you mean?"

I didn't like this. Morgan was toying with me, not fighting. He was enjoying this.

"Yeah," I said, "my brother. I hear you got him."

"Well, you heard wrong, punk. I don't got him. He's out there somewhere getting' his dick sucked by my old lady. When I find him, and I will find him, he's not gonna have a dick left to suck. You understand punk?"

I didn't answer.

"Hey! Answer a simple question," he said. "Maybe this'll help." Morgan drew back his right hand, already in a tight fist and swung fast into the left side of my face. My head snapped to the side. Vanelli and friend kept me from falling. I shook my head, trying to clear my eyes. I had blood in my mouth and my left ear had an echo in it.

I spit some blood on the ground. "Where's Ronnie Birch?"

"No, no, punk," Morgan said, " answer my question first. You understand what I'm gonna to do to your brother?"

"I understand," I said.

Morgan smiled. He reached up and patted my face, almost like he was congratulating a kid for getting good grades. Then he put his left fist into my stomach, hard. I tried to pull my knees up, but it didn't work. A sharp pain moved from my stomach to my neck.

"Now, where were we?" he said. "Ah, yes, Mr. Birch. Well, he had an appointment and couldn't be with us this morning. I'm grateful that he arranged this meeting." All three of them laughed. "But Tony didn't give him much choice, did you Tony?"

Vanelli shook his head.

Morgan inhaled some smoke and, of course, blew it in my face. "So let me tell you why I called this meeting," Morgan said, still enjoying himself. "I'm a man of honor. I may be a crook, but when I give my word, I keep it. Do you get me?"

I didn't answer, so Tony yanked on my arm, hard. I nodded my head.

"You, on the other hand, you lied to me, motherfucker." Morgan was angry now. "You gave me your word that fuck-ass was clean." I saw his fist coming, but I was held too tightly. I couldn't dodge it. I moved my head and took a hit below my left ear, on the neck. It stung, but if that was the toughest shot he could muster, I knew I'd make it. Good thing Vanelli wasn't doing the hitting.

"And I believed you, godamnit," he went on. "You gave me your word and I was sucker enough to believe you." Morgan telegraphed the next blow to my stomach. He missed my solar plexus, his fist glancing off my ribs. My legs went numb.

"I agree to leave the bastard alone. I left him alone 'cuz you said it was personal. So what do I do now, punk? Huh?" Morgan was standing six inches away, his face leaning into mine.

"What do I do? My wife leaves me this note, see, on the bed so I don't miss it. Tells me the good doctor is takin' her to paradise or some goddamn place." Morgan's knee came up and caught me in the groin.

"Ahhh," I yelled. I tried to double up, but Vanelli kept me standing. That one hurt. I gasped for air.

"Well, I'm giving you my word on this, punk," Morgan said. "When I find them, and I will find them, I'm going to cut his dick off myself. Then I'll kill him. I'll make him bleed, then I'll kill him." Morgan took a step backwards, put the cigar in his mouth. I knew what was coming. His left fist came into my stomach with a thud. Before I could react, the right fist caught my jaw again. Vanelli let go and I hit the ground. I heard Morgan say, "So long punk. Don't get in my away again or I'll let Tony have you." He kicked me hard, in the ribs, on the right side.

I lay curled up in a fetal position with my arms folded around my ribs. I opened my eyes just enough to see the three of them walk up the street and turn the corner. I spit some blood out of my mouth. I was hurt.

I stayed on the street for two or three minutes, then unwrapped my arms and slowly sat up and leaned against the car. My midsection ached, but there was no sharp pain, so he didn't break any ribs. I felt my face. It was cut and bleeding. I felt woozy, unsteady. My keys were still in my jacket pocket. I got them out, reached up and unlocked the door. I left the key in the lock. I moved to all fours. My stomach hardened. I waited until the nausea passed. Using the car, I slowly got to my feet, opened the door, grabbed the key and sat down inside. I swung my feet in, closed the door and turned the key. That took a long time, or so it seemed.

Driving was tougher than I thought it would be. Stiff and sore was bad enough, but my head pounded, and my eyes were cloudy. Fortunately, the morning rush hour hadn't started yet. I saw a hint of light on the horizon when I pulled into the garage. I rode the elevator to the fourth floor.

Ellen sat up on the couch when I walked in. "Frank!" she said startled. "What happened? Come on, sit down."

She walked me to the couch. I didn't resist. I took off the sweatshirt. I was soaked with sweat and the blood on my face was starting to harden.

Ellen brought me a plastic bag filled with ice. "Here," she said. I held it to the left side of my face, mostly on my jaw. I talked, slowly, about Morgan.

"Do you think Ronnie Birch set you up? Would he do that?"

"Don't know. I've known him a long time. Maybe they didn't give him any choice. I'll find out. He's number one on my list of things to do today." I rearranged the ice bag and put it back after Ellen wiped my face with a warm cloth.

"You're positive that Morgan said Clare told him that she was skipping town with Tom?"

"Yes. He told me she left a note where he wouldn't miss it."

"He obviously didn't, miss it," Ellen said. She took the ice bag and carefully wiped the rest of my face and neck with the warm cloth.

As we talked, a few things became clear. For one thing, Clare had built a clever plan. For another, she'd intentionally told her husband that she was leaving.

"She had a good reason to tell him," Ellen said. "And it had nothing to do with an extramarital affair."

"What then?" I asked. "Revenge?"

"No. Getting away. Getting away from a man who has the resources and determination to hunt her down."

"So poor Tommy really is irrelevant."

Ellen nodded. "She just used him to build an escape plan."

"And Clare diverted attention from her getaway by forcing Morgan to concentrate on Tommy."

"But you were first," Ellen said.

"Just like Jacque said."

"Just like Jacque said," Ellen nodded again. "Clare's flown the coop. Morgan wasn't looking for her tonight. Or Tommy. He was beating the shit out of you instead."

I sighed and rubbed my sore jaw. The ice helped. The ache was subsiding. But by afternoon, my jaw would be swollen, ice or no ice.

Ellen left to get ready for work and I turned on the shower. I stood under the hottest water I could stand. It helped sooth my nervous system and maybe the aches, too. No matter how often I read that people, men in particular, can handle this kind of punishment, it still takes days for my system to readjust, to function without twitching, to move without pain.

I dried off and put on the terrycloth robe that Ellen wore this morning. I had time for a short nap before going to the office. I lay on the couch and pulled the collar of the robe up around my neck. It smelled like Ellen. I drifted off to sleep knowing that Tommy was the target now. And I had no idea where he was.

CHAPTER 15

I finished a third cup of coffee and looked at my watch. It was 9:30. I felt like I'd been up all night.

Paying careful attention to my wardrobe, I chose a gray worsted wool suit, blue button down shirt, a print tie and black wing tips. I needed to look and feel as professional as possible. Skirmishes in the street were not part of my job description. I knew I could handle questions from my colleagues at the office, but it was just hard to accept the fact that helping my brother had turned so ugly.

Not to mention the people involved. Jacque and Ellen were right. Clare planned this whole escapade. Meeting Tommy wasn't intentional, but using him in her scheme certainly was.

I poured the last of the coffee in the sink and rinsed the carafe. I grabbed my suit coat and stopped in the bathroom. Looking in the mirror didn't help my face any. The swollen lip was noticeable, but better than I expected. The left side of my face, however, was scraped, bruised and two distinct scabs had started to form. I'm not sure that wing tips will help today.

I waited for the elevator without protest. Outside, the fresh air felt good. It must have been 55 degrees and the sun was up. My muscles loosened up as I walked to Sheridan Road and caught a cab to the office.

At the reception desk, Rose said, "Good morning, Mr. Marshall. Jacque picked up your messages." Then she stared at my damaged face. I detected a faint smile. "Did we have a difficult evening?" she asked.

"Mice," I said. The expression on Rose's face turned quizzical. "I beg your pardon?"

"The mice in my building are something else. When they attack in the middle of the night, well..." I tried to smile, but my face hurt.

In the office, Jacque was on the phone. She looked up and dropped the receiver on the desk. She never took her eyes off me, but picked up the phone and said, "Dorothy, I'll call you back. Mr. Marshall just walked in." She stood up. "Frank! What happened to you?"

"Come on in," I said, pointing. "We've got some work to do."

There was some ice in the small refrigerator next to my desk, and I put it in a heavy plastic bag. "I remember when I used to do this for sore leg muscles," I said, holding the bag against my face. Then I began to tell Jacque about my evening with Rick Morgan.

"I know the first job this morning," she said, "find Ronnie Birch or Dr. Marshall."

"It's both. But finding Ronnie will be easier. I'll start with him. See if you can get any information on Tommy's whereabouts. Call the University first."

"Is Dr. Marshall in bad trouble?" Jacque asked apprehensively.

"Morgan made it quite clear," I said, accepting the obvious, "that Tommy's number one on his shit list now that he's done with me."

Jacque left and I picked up the phone, punched in the Tribune's number and asked for Ronnie's desk. "This is Birch," the voice said, "maybe you'll hear from me, maybe you won't."

"This is Marshall," I said to the answering machine. I looked at my watch. "It's 11:30. I want to talk with you. Pronto. You got that? Then I'll decide if you're a sonovabitch or not." I hung up, reached into my brief bag and took out my Franklin Planner. I looked in the phone directory for Ronnie's name. I got his office number, home number and address. I called home. He answered.

"It's Frank Marshall, Ronnie. We need to talk."

"Frank, I'm sorry," he started, but I interrupted him.

"In person, Ronnie. No argument. Get your ass to my office and do it now. Got it?"

"On my way, Frank."

Jacque had no luck with the University of Chicago. "The secretary in the History Department said it's policy not to discuss faculty. She suggested I try University Relations. That's the PR wing."

"I'll run over there after I have a chat with Ronnie," I said. "Maybe they'll be less hesitant to talk to his brother."

"I'll run down planes, trains and busses." Jacque said. "Somehow, I can't imagine Clare Morgan or Dr. Marshall on a bus. Flying the Concorde, on the other hand," she added with a slight grin, "is another ballgame entirely."

Smiling still hurt. I picked up the ice bag and put it back on my sore jaw.

It didn't take Ronnie Birch long to show up. Jacque followed him into my office and they both sat down. I stayed in my seat and didn't offer my hand. He didn't look good. He wasn't marked up like me, but his pale skin was almost gray. His thinning hair needed brushing and his mustache trimming. His dark brown suit took up more room in the chair than he did. This was not a confident man. And he was nervous. He reached into his jacket pocket and pulled out a flattened pack of Marlboros.

"Ronnie," I said, holding my right hand out in front of me like a traffic cop. "Not in here."

"Shit, Frank," he said. "I fuckin' forgot you quit these things years ago." Ronnie suddenly remembered that Jacque was in the office, too. He looked over his shoulder and saw her. "Ah, sorry, Miss. Sometimes I cuss too much." Jacque nodded at Ronnie and smiled demurely as if she'd never heard a four-letter word in her life.

"So, what happened, Ronnie?" I asked.

"Your face looks sore," he said. "Are you okay?"

"Cut the crap, Ronnie. I took a beating because of you and I want to know why."

He nodded. "Sure, Frank. Did Vanelli do that?"

"No, goddamnit!" I said, loud. "Do you think I'd be sitting with you if he did? It was Morgan. I was lucky he wanted revenge himself or I'd be in the hospital, or worse." I was losing my patience. "Talk to me, Ronnie."

"Frank, I'm sorry. I really am. Morgan got me, too. I mean, I was dumb enough to believe him when he called in the middle of the night. Said he had proof, written proof, about who killed Councilman Wetstein." Jacob Wetstein had resigned from City Council during a money scandal. He was found strangled in Grant Park two years ago. "I guess I wanted to believe he had the missing piece I needed." Ronnie had broken more stories about the city's major crimes than any other reporter. "I worked every angle of that story for a year before it dried up."

I believed him. "How'd they get you to call me?"

"Morgan picked me up in his limo about 3 A.M. In front of my building. Vanelli was with him and some other big guy I didn't recognize. You see the other guy, Frank?" I nodded. "I was sittin' between Morgan and Vanelli. The other guy drove."

"The phone call, Ronnie?"

"Yeah, well, um… it's kinda hard to talk about, you know what I mean?" He looked over his shoulder at Jacque. She smiled. I nodded at Jacque.

"Mr. Birch," she said. The smile was gone, and her voice was all business. "I've spent my entire life listening to language worse than yours, so cut the shit and tell us what happened, or I will personally throw your ass out of this office." Ronnie was impressed. Me, too. "You set Frank up, and you'd better have a helluva good reason."

"Frank, I've never been so scared in my life. They wanted me to get you down to the park. I didn't buy the threats at first, but then…" his voice trailed off. "Morgan said he was gonna cut my pecker off if I didn't call you, Frank." He looked at Jacque again.

"Continue, Mr. Birch," she said.

"Well, I... I didn't believe him. Everybody says shit like that. But that's all it is. Bullshit. I told Morgan to go fuck himself. He didn't like that." Ronnie was sweating across the top of his forehead. I dropped a box of Kleenex on the desk in front of him. He took two tissues, wiping his forehead and the left side of his face.

"Then Morgan told Vanelli to cut it off," he said. "Jesus, Frank. Before I knew what hit me, my pants are down to my fuckin' knees. Vanelli pulls out this knife, a switchblade, and grabs my cock with his other hand. I still didn't believe he'd do it. Morgan gave me another chance to say yes. I shook my head, and Vanelli slit the skin on the top of my pecker. He did. Can you fuckin' believe it? You want to see the bandage?"

I shook my head.

"No, I guess not."

"Then what did you do?" My voice was softer now. It was a question, not a demand.

"I made the call," Ronnie said with a shrug. He had tears in the corners of his eyes. "Never been that scared, Frank. Honest to God."

"You want some coffee, Ronnie?" I asked. He nodded and Jacque went to get him a cup. We sat quietly while Ronnie sipped the coffee.

"I owe you, Frank. We've known each other a long time. Helped each other lots of times." He looked at me with honest regret. "You shouldn't take a beating on account of me."

"You were in a tough place," I said gently.

"What do you need, Frank?" he asked. "Some help with Morgan? Whatever you need."

"Find out where Clare Morgan and my brother went. It's somewhere out of the country. Europe, probably."

"I'll find 'em for you, Frank. Maybe I can get some other info at the same time."

"That would help, Ronnie." We talked for a few more minutes, then he left. I had mixed feelings about what happened, but I felt better knowing that he was forced to call. I like the guy and I hated the idea of him being that scared.

Sometimes I wonder," Jacque said softly, "sometimes I wonder if the city makes people treat people that way, or are some people just sonofabitches like Rick Morgan."

I shook my head.

"You know, I love this city. First came here when I was a little girl. The buildings, the lake, all of it. I love it. I came back after college. Wouldn't want to live anywhere else. Men like Morgan would be mean wherever they lived. It's about power. Violence gets them power and helps them keep it. A city has more men like Vanelli. Men who hire out their fists. It'd never occur to me to leave the city because of this, but it just makes me wonder if cities do that to people."

"I don't know," I said. "I feel bad for Ronnie. But I'm having a tougher time justifying my brother's behavior in all of this."

"But, Frank," Jacque said. "Dr. Marshall is going to need your help, more than ever now."

"I know, I know. I'm just pissed at him right now, that's all. His adolescent behavior gets people hurt."

"He's your brother. You can't let him go it alone."

"I'm not going to let him hang, Jacque," I said, "but, goddamit, he's got to take some responsibility for all of this. At least Clare has a motive. She wants to get away from Morgan. But what's Tommy's reason? To hear him tell it, he has a god-given right to get laid on a regular basis. What the hell kind of reason is that?"

Jacque shrugged her shoulders.

Further discussion about Tommy would get us nowhere, so I decided to see what I could find out about Professor Marshall at the University of Chicago.

CHAPTER 16

The Department of History is housed in Chumsley Hall, built during the days when Abe Lincoln was president. The five-floor structure looks like a movie set with faded red bricks and dark green ivy covering the building. All romantic visions of higher education fly out of the window, however, in the department's main office. Most of the work done in the last 100 years was strictly cosmetic and tacky. New linoleum covers old pine floors, veneer paneling lines the walls, and office cubicles add more spaces for more people. It helps about as much as lipstick on a corpse.

I walked to the counter just inside the main office door. It looked like the video rental at Jacobson's Drug Store. Maybe I should rent a Betamax copy of *Romancing the Stone* while I'm here.

"May I help you, sir?" said a woman in her mid-thirties. She wore a denim jumpsuit with a red cotton shirt underneath. Taking off her glasses, she stood up and walked to the counter.

"My name is Frank Marshall," I said, and handed her my card. "I'm Professor Thomas Marshall's brother. I haven't been able to contact Tom for several days, and I thought you might be able to help me find him."

"Well, Mr.," she hesitated and looked at my card, "Mr. Marshall. It's our policy not to discuss the activities of our faculty."

"This is strictly personal," I said. "It has nothing to do with his work for the University." She wasn't moved by my rationale. "In fact, it's quite urgent that I find him."

She looked at the card again. "Hold on a second, okay?" She turned and walked to a door at the rear of the room. She knocked and walked in.

I looked at the wall to my right. It was filled with rows of mail slots for the faculty and graduate assistants. Most of them were empty. A handwritten memo announcing a meeting was taped to the edge of the boxes.

"Mr. Marshall," the secretary said, "would you come this way, please?" She gestured towards the door in back. "Our Chairperson, Stephanie Anderson, would like to see you."

I followed her into the office. "Mr. Marshall, this is Dr. Anderson." Chairperson Anderson stood in front of her desk. She was in her mid-fifties and about five-feet seven inches tall. She wore a beige wool suit, man-tailored and a navy cotton shirt open at the neck. Probably very chic in the halls of the academy. I extended my hand. She took it. Her grip was very firm and business-like.

"Dr. Anderson," I said, "Thank you for seeing me."

"You're welcome," she said, "sit down, please." I took the only chair in front of the desk. It was made of blond wood and matched her desk. Very 1950s. The office was small and every inch of wall space was occupied by bookshelves, floor to ceiling.

There were two large windows, one on either side of her desk. A large wool rag rug in faded grays and blues covered much of the wood floor. This was likely a charming office a very long time ago. Now it was shabby.

"Mr. Marshall," she said, "may I ask why you are making inquiries into the personal life of a member of the University's faculty?"

"Certainly." I wondered if she always used so many words to ask a question. "Tom Marshall has been my brother longer than he's been Professor Marshall. I think he may be in some trouble, and I've not been able to get in touch with him."

"I see," she said, leaning forward, resting her elbows on the desk. "Mr. Marshall, please don't misunderstand our intent. When Ms. Hodges"—she pointed to the outer office—" told you that University policy prohibits discussing the lives of our faculty, she was acting in the best interests of Dr. Marshall, as well as doing her job."

"Which is to keep guys like me from snooping around?"

"Something like that."

"Dr. Anderson, if I could convince you that Tom Marshall's best interests were also being served by telling me what you know, would you be willing to, shall we say, overlook University policy?"

"Mr. Marshall, I doubt that there's anything of sufficient import that you could say that would make me violate the responsibility bestowed upon me by the University's provost."

I didn't have anything to lose, so I sat up straight in my chair and pretended that I had to convince the teacher that I knew the right answer. "Let me tell you what I know and what I think has happened," I said. "Tom Marshall got involved with a married woman and some pretty nasty people, the kind of people who break knees when they're not watching college football. My face used to be a lot prettier until some of those people didn't like the idea that I was trying to help him out of a jam."

"Might not the same people who did that"—she pointed at my face—"continue to object to your ongoing involvement in Professor Marshall's affairs?"

"Probably, but somebody has to help him," I said. "My guess is that he's been gone for a while. He may have left without telling you or anyone else what he had planned. These are not nice people, Dr. Anderson. Tom needed secrecy to get away, and now he needs me."

I tried to read her face, but there was no visible reaction to what I'd just told her. She said nothing. I leaned forward. "Look, Dr. Anderson, I'll find Tom with or without your help. You can help me find him faster before he gets hurt or killed."

That got a reaction. Her shoulders dropped.

"Is it really that bad?"

I nodded.

She hesitated, but not for long. "He's been gone for two weeks. You were right. He just vanished. Not a word. He missed several classes before we could get a temporary faculty person in here to cover his classes."

"Had Tom been acting differently in the days before he disappeared?" I asked. She shook her head.

She went on to confirm what I already suspected. Tom had little contact with her or other faculty unless it was to complain about teaching conditions and skimpy raises. That was the same adolescent manner he used to complain about not getting Bulls' tickets.

Before I left, I assured the Chairperson of the History Department that her setting aside of University policy had been most helpful. But I was going to need a break if I was going to find Tommy before Rick Morgan did.

CHAPTER 17

The wind off Lake Michigan slapped my face. It hit the sweat on my chest right though a faded long-sleeved T-shirt that said, "Clinton-Gore-'92." Even my legs were chilled in the November wind.

My face had healed just fine in the five weeks since Rick Morgan tried to rearrange it. But there was no word on the whereabouts of the romantic duo, and I never stopped worrying that Morgan would find them before I did. My usual sources were of no help.

I turned out of Lincoln Park at St. Joseph's Hospital and headed up Oakdale. I walked the last two blocks to keep my leg muscles loose.

The phone was ringing when I opened the door. I picked up the receiver from the wall phone in the kitchen.

"Good morning, Frank." It was Jacque. "Glad I caught you." "Ronnie Birch called a few minutes ago. Says he's got something for you."

"Did he say what?"

"Nope. He wants to talk to you ASAP. He'll be at the *Tribune* 'till noon.'"

After a hot shower, I made some coffee, sat down on the living room couch, punched in the *Tribune's* number and asked for Ronnie's desk.

"This is Birch," he said.

"It's Frank. Jacque told me you've got some news."

"Damn straight, I do. Of course it's not exactly what you were lookin' for, but it might help." He'd been talking to his sources about Tommy and Clare. Like everybody else asking questions, he got no answers. "But yesterday I was talking to Weasel Wayne. Do you know Weasel, Frank?"

"I don't know anyone named Weasel, Ronnie," I said. "You've been reading too many slick novels."

"Shit, Frank," he said, "I only read the fuckin' newspapers, you know that. Would I make up a name like that?" Ronnie described Weasel as an aging, small time bookie who'd run over a baby carriage for another bet.

"I'm placing a bet yesterday," Ronnie said, "when Weasel mentions Morgan's old lady. Did I still want information, he asked? I said yes. Told me he didn't know about the broad, but he had heard Morgan high-tailed it to Europe."

"Europe." That had been one of my first guesses weeks ago. "Can you trust this guy, Ronnie? Is he on the level?"

"Sort of, Frank," he said. "But it doesn't make any difference because I checked it out. I know a couple of guys who know some guys who work for Morgan. They said Morgan and Vanelli left the country."

"That's a start," I said. "We need to try the airlines.'

"One up on you, babe. This is payback time, remember. My niece is a travel agent. She checked. Morgan and Vanelli flew Air France from O'Hare to DeGaulle four days ago. Used their own names."

"Paris?"

"Yep," he said. "Gay Paree. I don't know about you, Frank, but I just can't see Morgan and Vanelli strolling down the Champs Elysees. Know what I mean? So why do you think they went to Paris so suddenly, huh?"

"Because our romantic couple is hiding there."

"Must be!"

"Say, Ronnie. Do you think your niece could check to see if Clare and Tommy went to Paris, too?"

"No luck, Frank," he said. "She looked. Also London, Rome and Amsterdam for two weeks or so about the time they disappeared. Of course, they could have used phony names. Getting passports wouldn't be a problem for Morgan's wife."

"Thanks, my friend," I said. "I'll be in touch." I hung up the phone and sipped some coffee. Paris. How the hell could they expect to hide in Paris? Of course, maybe they weren't in the city, just flew there. But somebody must have spotted them since Morgan took off so quickly. At least it was something to go on.

I wanted to brainstorm, so I called Ellen at her office. She was out, so I left a message. This was a day for khakis, a blue oxford cloth button-down shirt and a burgundy cotton crew-neck sweater. I grabbed a navy blazer, just in case.

"Paris," Jacque said. "Wouldn't it be easier to hide in a small town in Iowa?"

"For all we know, they tried that," I said. "But how long would either one of them last in a cornfield? Be tough to get a good cup of espresso."

Jacque handed me a small stack of mail. "By the way," she said, "the Chairperson of the History Department, a Professor Anderson, called. She wants to see you." Jacque smiled. "I made an appointment for you at two this afternoon."

I was sorting the mail when Ellen called me back. I told her I needed help and wanted Jacque to join us for dinner at Bellino's. In the meantime, I would find out what Professor Anderson had to say.

In a world that's always changing, it's nice to know some things never change. Particularly the look and feel of a college campus. I took my time walking to Chumsley Hall. When I got to the counter in the History Department, the same woman was behind her desk. She didn't see me come in and continued typing away on a shabby olive green Selectric. "Good morning," I said.

She looked up from the typewriter. Her eyes brightened. "I remember you," she said. "I'll tell Professor Anderson you're here."

"Ah, Ms?" I hesitated, hoping she'd fill in the gap.

"Hodges," she said, "Wendy Hodges."

"Ms. Hodges, I haven't seen a Selectric in a long time. No computer?"

A wry smile moved across her face. "The budget," she said, "the budget."

Professor Anderson met me at her office door. Her hair still needed a decent brushing, but she looked quite professional in a man-tailored navy suit with a white cotton turtleneck under the jacket. I sat in the same chair and she took up her place behind the desk. She made a point of telling me that she was less concerned about University policy than during our last talk. I wondered what changed her mind.

She handed me an envelope. It was one of those lightweight airmail envelopes with the colored borders. Opened it was stationery, folded, it became the envelope. The postmark was too light to read, but the stamps were French. I unfolded it and read the letter. It was from Tommy. He apologized for skipping out on his teaching and committee responsibilities. He pleaded for understanding because of, what he called, "serious family difficulties." He asked Anderson for an unpaid leave of absence. He didn't say when he'd be back or if he'd write again.

"Given what you told me earlier, Mr. Marshall, I assume the difficulties he refers to are more serious than he makes them sound. However childishly he behaves sometimes, Professor Marshall has never walked away from his professional responsibilities. I think he needs help that neither the University nor I can provide. That's why I called you."

"I'm glad you did," I said. "I haven't had any luck finding him, I'm sorry to say. This helps." I looked at the letter. "Can he get a leave of absence like that? Just by asking?"

"Certainly not," she answered. "Any faculty member can get two unpaid leaves in two years. But the person requesting the leave must fill out the forms ahead of time. I cannot do it for him."

"Can he lose his job because of this?"

"Perhaps," she said. "But not until I file the appropriate papers to begin disciplinary proceedings."

Something in the tone of her voice told me she didn't want to do that. "Would you have a problem giving me some time to sort this out," I asked, "before you file the papers?"

"Well, Mr. Marshall," she said, "as Department Chairperson, I'm obligated to uphold the policies of the University." She fidgeted in her seat and ran her fingers through her hair, twice. "But you can see by looking at this mess," she waved her hand over the surface of the desk, "that I've got a lot of work to do. It will take me a good two weeks, perhaps longer, before I could file those papers. You see my problem, don't you, Mr. Marshall?"

"I certainly do," I said, nodding my head. "I'll call you as soon as I know something."

"Thank you. I would be most appreciative."

I left the halls of academe feeling uneasy. The letter helped verify that Tommy was in France, likely in Paris. It helped that Anderson was willing to bend the rules to give me some time. But assuming I find Tommy alive and unhurt, am I really helping him if I bail him out? Tommy had to grow up sooner or later. A man in his forties has to face the consequences of his behavior.

It was no use. As long as Rick Morgan's chasing him, I'm in Tommy's life whether he likes it or not.

I spent the rest of the day working on other matters for the firm. Since Tommy's troubles surfaced, it was hard to remember that my employer was Winkler, Norton and Barger, not Professor Marshall. However understanding the partners may be about my extracurricular activities, I still had work to do.

Jacque had still had no luck tracking down Tommy and Clare. She even tried the Cunard Line in case they'd tried to throw Morgan off the scent by sailing the high seas. No luck there either. I was convinced that they used aliases. Meaning bogus passports. Clare's offer of two-hundred grand clearly showed she had enough money to buy passports. The tricky part was that the source for the phony documents would have to be a Rick Morgan connection. Could she also have bought silence? Or would some guy figure that he'd take her money, then sell what he knew to Morgan who would pay big bucks for the information?

I did what I could on my other cases. Fortunately the workload wasn't that heavy or complicated. Maybe the approaching holiday season had something to do with it. I told Jacque to meet Ellen and me at Bellino's.

"Is this a working dinner, Frank?"

"It is indeed. I'm buying."

Bellino's. One of our favorite restaurants. It doesn't hold the emotional attachment that Medici does, but it's a good place to eat. We avoid the long waits of the weekends and meet after work instead. It's a big barn of a place, an old warehouse, in fact. But room dividers and the arrangement of the tables create a comfortable feeling.

I gave the woman at the maitre d' stand Ellen Paxton's name and she escorted me to a table on the landing where Ellen was sipping a glass of white wine.

"Hello, sweetheart," I said, as I leaned over and kissed her. "I'm always amazed at how sexy you look after a hard day at the office."

"Oh, please, Frank," she said, drawing out the word, "please." "This is just another two-piece suit. You'd think an ankle-length rain slicker was sexy if I had it on."

"Only if the slicker's yellow," I said, with a straight face.

"You're impossible. Jacque's coming, I take it?"

"In a few minutes. How's Wall Street today?"

"Mixed. The Dow was off two points, but advances led declines twelve to nine at the close. The NASDAQ closed up a point and a half. Should I go on?"

"Not if you keep rattling off numbers. Maybe I should ask about the latest offer from New York instead." I wondered how much longer the home office would try to get her to move. Seven offers in three years. Flattering. But she's always chosen Chicago and me.

"They upped the ante again," she admitted. "I've got to say that it gets tougher with each offer."

The waiter arrived and I ordered a scotch rocks. Ellen pointed at her nearly empty wine glass. We scanned the menu as we talked. I told her about Tommy's letter to the History Department and Morgan's sudden departure for the City of Light.

"You really think they're in Paris?"

I shrugged.

"Is there any way you can find out for sure?"

"Jacque's working on it," I said. "Ronnie Birch, too. They're obviously trying to stay out of sight."

"That's what I'd do if Morgan was after me," Ellen said. "But how can they hide in a big city like that? Surely, there's a French branch of the Mafia that would look for them."

I rolled my eyes at the mention of the Mafia. I started to say something when Jacque walked up to the table.

"Hello, Ellen, Frank," she said. "I need a draft."

Before sitting down, she dropped a large, flat envelope-like package in front of me. It said FedEx across the top. It was an overseas delivery.

"It arrived just as I was leaving. Oh, and Ronnie Birch called. He said to tell you that Morgan and Vanelli checked into the Hotel Meurice in Paris."

Ellen started to laugh. "Well, that's fitting."

Jacque and I looked at each other, stumped.

Ellen shook her head in mock frustration. "History," she said. "World War II. You've heard of it, haven't you?"

Sarcasm is a wonderful thing.

"The Hotel Meurice was Nazi headquarters when the Germans occupied Paris. General von Cholitz was in a suite at the Meurice when he disobeyed Hitler's order to burn the city just before the Allies liberated it. Anyway, I think it's ironic that a sweet guy like Morgan picked the old Nazi headquarters, that's all."

"You have a bizarre sense of humor, you know," I said.

The waiter brought Jacque's beer and asked if we were ready to order. I sent him away. I was too interested in the envelope to think about food. I ripped open the flap and emptied the contents on the table. Three pieces of paper, each standard letter size, fell out. I looked inside.

"That's it," I said. One sheet of paper was hand written. I read it first. "It's from Tommy." I read aloud, "'Clare left me two days ago. She's not coming back. She took the passports we had made. Morgan's here. He and some big guy are looking for me. I'm okay, for now. Frank, I need your help. I don't know what to do. But I wouldn't blame you if you say no.'"

"What are the other pages?" Ellen asked. I looked them over quickly. They were computer printouts. Reservation forms.

"Apparently, I have a room waiting for me at a place called the Grand Hotel de Balcons. In Paris, of course. I've also got a seat, paid for, on United flight 316 leaving O'Hare for DeGaulle."

The waiter did a walk-by of our table and thought better than to ask.

"Well," I said, "now we know."

"Wonder what'll turn up next?" Jacque asked, not seriously.

"So the cast of characters in this little drama has migrated to Paris," Ellen said. She looked at me. "And you're about to join them."

"Why did he send reservations?" Jacque asked. "Why not call and tell you what happened?"

I didn't have an answer for that one, but Ellen did.

"Rejection," she said. "He probably figured Frank would blow up on the telephone and refuse to go." She had a point. "Tougher to say no if you've got reservations in your hands."

"Life runs on Tommy's terms," I said, "or he tries to make it so."

"Boy, he must be desperate," Jacque said.

"Well, Morgan made it clear that Tommy would pay," I said. "I'd feel desperate, too, if I were in his shoes. Must feel really alone now that Clare has ditched him."

We ordered dinner, finally making the waiter happy, but I'd pretty much lost my appetite.

"I'm pissed at Clare Morgan," Ellen said. "I told you that she had a scheme to get away from her husband. Dumping Tommy after they left the country had to be part of the plan all along. She must know that Morgan's in Paris, too."

None of us ate much food. I could tell that Ellen was not enthusiastic about my impending European trip.

Jacque picked up the reservation forms. "I'll double check these first thing," she said. "It's getting late."

After Jacque left, I said to Ellen, "You're not hot for me to go to Paris, are you sweetheart?"

"You will go, then?"

"Yes."

"I know," she said, "I know. Let's drop it for now, okay? It's been a long day and I'm tired."

I smiled and squeezed her hand. "Come to my place?"

"Of course," she said. "What I don't get, Frank... what's the point? What good is it going to do to bail him out? He's got to learn that actions have consequences. You could get hurt again, and for what? He'll just end up in another mess."

"You're probably right, but this mess could get him dead," I said. "What am I supposed to do? Leave him out there to die?"

CHAPTER 18

I heard a noise. What was it? I couldn't make it out.

"Turn that thing off, Frank," Ellen said. She sounded like she had cotton in her mouth.

My arm came from under the covers, moved in a sweeping arc and landed on the top of the clock radio.

"Thank you, dear." Ellen rolled over in my direction, leaned against me and draped an arm over my chest. I put my arm around her shoulder.

"You feel wonderful," I said, barely awake. "Got a tough day?" Ellen snuggled her body close to mine. Her fingers began walking up my leg. They paused momentarily at hip level. I wondered which direction they'd take next.

"Not really," she said. "Two guys from the New York office are in town. Jack Shields is okay. Norm Kingston's a pain in the neck. Thinks all women are sex goddesses."

"Sounds good to me," I said, stretching out the word "good."

Slap! Ellen hit my stomach with her hand.

"Ouch. Is that any way to treat the man who made mad, passionate love to you last night?"

She lifted herself onto one elbow. I looked at her, and we laughed.

Ellen threw back the covers and got out of bed. She walked backwards out of the room towards the bathroom, making sure

I got a good look. I watched intently then said, just before she disappeared, "I'll make the coffee."

Ellen was in the shower by the time I reached the kitchen. I'd finished pouring water into the Mr. Coffee when the phone rang. I looked at my watch. It read 6:23. I picked up the receiver of the wall phone. It was Tommy, in Paris. He talked so fast that I had little chance to respond. It must be close to noon in France. Most of what he said didn't make much sense. A lot of gibberish about Clare and Morgan and money. He mentioned a "big guy" whom I took to mean Tony Vanelli.

"Tommy," I said, trying to interrupt. "Tommy. Wait a minute, will you?"

He did.

"Look, Tom, take it one step at a time. Have you been drinking?"

"Jess a little, Frank." His voice was thick. "Martinis, I think."

"Where are you? Are you in a safe place?"

"Yesh," he said, "at my hotel. Same one for you. Don't say it." I understood the mixed up words to mean that he didn't want to say the name of the hotel. It was the same hotel where I am to stay.

"Are you coming, Frank?"

I took a deep breath. "Yes, Tom, I'll be there. What's going on?"

He started to cry. Not loud, but I could hear it in his voice. "She's gone, Frank," he said softly. "Clare's gone. What am I gonna do?"

I saw Ellen standing at the kitchen door, toweling her hair. She had my white terrycloth robe on again. I pointed at the coffee. She poured two mugs full. I moved the receiver away from my mouth and whispered, "Tommy." She nodded and took a sip of coffee, then walked into the living room and sat on the couch. She didn't look happy.

Tommy tried his best to give me the story, but the booze and his emotional state made it hard to follow. I listened for a long time. He only mentioned Morgan once. He was too wrapped up in lost love.

"Are you going to meet me at the airport, Tom?" I asked.

His answer was confused.

"Okay, I'll see you at the hotel, then." I put the receiver back on the wall hook. I took my coffee to the living room and sat down next to Ellen. The coffee tasted strong.

Ellen put her mug on the table in front of us. "What'd he say?"

"He was a little drunk, but apparently Clare split after a few weeks. He hadn't heard from her until she called to warn him that Morgan was in Paris. He's hiding out in a small hotel on the Left Bank."

"Correct me if I'm wrong," Ellen said slowly, " but Tom Marshall is at best a fool and at worst an asshole."

I nodded, reluctantly.

"And it's long past the time that he took responsibility for the shit he gets into."

I nodded again.

"You can't keep saving him. It'll catch up with him eventually."

"This isn't the right time."

"Damnit, Frank," she said, raising her voice. "It's never the right time. You know that. This is as good a time as any."

"This time could get him dead, Ellen," I said, raising my voice, too. "At the very least, Morgan's going to hurt him."

"So what? There, I've said it. So what? I don't want you to get hurt again. It won't work anyway. Tommy doesn't deserve it."

"He doesn't deserve to get what Morgan wants to give him," I said, easier, trying to lower the heat.

She wasn't giving up. "Can't you see what these people are? Morgan beat you up, Clare's used everybody within reach to get away from him, and Tommy's your brother, but he lies to you. You don't need this. He doesn't deserve it. You don't deserve it." She was standing now and had moved to the other side of the coffee table, facing me. "Give me one good reason why you should go to Paris?" she said. "Just one."

"Because he's my brother, that's why," I said. I was standing now, too.

"That's not good enough, goddamnit. Not any more."

"It is for me," I said. "It is for me."

She turned and walked away. I went to the kitchen and poured more coffee. In a minute she was back, dressed in my sweats, black pants and a bright red shirt with the outline of the state of Michigan on the front. She carried her clothes from yesterday over her arm.

"Look, Frank," she said. "I don't tell you how to do your business, you don't tell me how to do mine. But this... this scares me. We're supposed to spend the Thanksgiving holiday with my parents in Petoskey, remember? Maybe some skiing if northern Michigan gets an early snow. Fun stuff, you know? You're acting like you're John Wayne, like you're the hero in some damn movie. It's about time Tommy learned to take care of himself."

I couldn't think of anything to say. "I'd like it if you'd take me to the airport. . ." I said, but I could see the answer on her face.

"I've got a full calendar. You'd better take a cab." She picked up her purse and walked to the door.

"I'll call you when I get back."

Ellen closed the door behind her without saying a word.

CHAPTER 19

I chose a very conservative gray pin-stripped suit, blue shirt and paisley tie. I needed to fit in, attorney style, when I told the boss that I wanted a week off to go to Paris. It'd be easier if Tommy were a client of the firm. But I had a few vacation days left. I'd been saving them for Thanksgiving weekend with Ellen's family.

"Maybe I shouldn't count on Thanksgiving," I said aloud to the empty apartment.

Ellen and I seldom disagree about our professional lives. And while I understand that she's worried, she also questioned my judgment about helping Tommy.

I walked down to Sheridan to catch a cab. The air was heavy. A cold rain couldn't be far off.

Jacque handed me the mail and my messages. I flipped through the stack hoping for a message from Ellen. I didn't see one. "Will you call Winkler's office and get me twenty minutes, ASAP," I asked her. Then I sat at my desk and stared out the window.

Jacque walked in and sat down. "You okay?"

"Is it that obvious?"

She nodded.

I told her about Tommy's call and what Ellen had said.

"She's got a point, Frank."

I looked at her, hard.

"I didn't say she was right... there isn't a right or wrong here... but you ought to try to see it from Ellen's perspective, that's all."

I let her suggestion pass.

"Did you check the reservations?"

"Yep. Both reservations check out," she said. "I called United and I got Betty Douglas—do you know Betty in accounting?"

I shook my head.

"Well, Betty speaks fluent French. She called the hotel. It was late afternoon over there."

"What about Winkler?" I asked.

"He's busy all morning," she said. "He can see you for ten minutes at noon."

I had plenty of things to take care of since I was going to be away for at least a week. Winkler was sure to ask if my work was covered, so I needed to talk to the attorneys in charge of my cases.

At noon, I walked down the hall, past the conference rooms and into Harold Winkler's office. Allison DeWolf, his executive assistant, was on the telephone. She waved. I sat down in one of three leather chairs that faced her desk.

"Hello, Frank," Allison said after she finished her call. "Go on in. He's expecting you."

I tapped Winkler's door lightly and walked in. His office was a dreamland to most of the associates. They want one just like it almost as much as they want a partnership in the firm. It was an enormous square with huge floor-to-ceiling windows on two sides. Winkler's desk was positioned at the corner, in front of the windows. There were a couch and chairs. Leather, of course. And a conference table with ten chairs. Bookcases lined the two other walls.

Winkler got up from his desk. "Hello, there, Frank. Let's sit over here." He gestured towards the couch. We shook hands and sat down.

Harold Winkler, third generation senior partner in the firm started by his grandfather, was 54 years old. He'd grown up in Chicago, and joined the firm as an associate the day after he finished law school at the University of Texas at Austin. He was tall, almost six-four, trim and very bald.

"I got a lunch meeting across town," he said, "so let's get right at it. What can I do for you?"

"I need a favor, Harold," I said. "My brother's in trouble, serious trouble I'm afraid, and I'm the only one he'll trust to help him."

"What kind of trouble?" Winkler asked. "Better yet, how serious?"

"My brother's a bit naïve. He got in over his head with some bad guys who could hurt him. I tried to get him out of it a while back, but it didn't work."

"Was that when your face turned black and blue?" Winkler asked. He had a reputation for not missing things.

I nodded.

"What do you need?"

"A week," I said. "Maybe ten days. I leave for Paris this afternoon. I've got a few vacation days and I'll take the rest without pay."

Winkler shook his head. "I don't care about the money, Frank. You do a good job for us. If you need to do this, do it. What's the status of your cases?"

"Fortunately, I only have three right now. There's Pat Longstreet's tax fraud case, and that's in negotiations with the IRS. Donald Solomon's handling the case, and he said I'm done with it barring something unexpected. West Bluff Realty is being sued by two of its former clients. All sides are taking depositions. Tracy Vincent's doing West Bluff and doesn't think she'll need me for two or three weeks. The only other matter I'm working on is Denise Kirshner, and she's your client."

Winkler laughed. "You certainly don't have to worry about Denise. I got a telegram from her last week. She's in Zurich with her young stud. So to speak." He laughed again. "They're going to Paris, too, as a matter of fact."

Winkler got out of his chair and so did I. "Frank, take the week," he said. "More if you need it. Just be careful if these guys play rough, all right?"

"I'll do that," I said. "Thanks."

"Give Allison your flight and hotel information in case we need to talk to you." I told him I would. We shook hands and Winkler said, "If I can help you out, let me know." I thanked him again.

I went back to my office and collected my brief bag. Jacque had gotten me a detailed map of Paris and $500 in French francs. I asked her to give Allison DeWolf my travel information. I called Ellen, but her secretary said she was in a meeting. I left a message.

"Good luck, Frank," Jacque said. "Take care of yourself, and call if I can do anything."

"Thanks."

I grabbed a cab on Michigan and went home to pack. I took mostly casual clothes, khakis, shirts, sweaters and a navy blazer. I stuffed my running gear in the bag just in case I had time and the inclination. I made sure I had my passport and credit cards. I tossed Robert B. Parker's latest Spenser novel in my brief bag for the plane ride.

I called for a cab. This wasn't a good time to get one on Sheridan. I tried Ellen's office one more time. She still wasn't available.

I sat quietly during the ride to O'Hare despite the cabby's repeated attempts to discuss the Bears' chances for a title. He finally figured out that I wasn't in the mood. I couldn't shake the argument with Ellen. I got out of the cab near the United Skycaps. I left my bag and went to the counter to check in. I still had an hour, so I found a quiet seat near my gate, took out the Spenser novel and opened it to chapter one.

United Air Lines flight 316, non-stop to Paris lifted off on time. I settled back and waited for the first wave of drinks and food. A scotch tasted especially nice and the food was reasonably good. They helped pass the time and ease some of the tension of the last few weeks. Many of the people around me were covering up with blankets for the night. A few people were watching the end of the flight's first film, Nora Efron's *Sleepless in Seattle*. I'd seen it on the ground some months before. I sipped some water and rearranged my head on the small pillow, turned out the overhead reading light and tried to doze off.

I couldn't get Ellen out of my mind. I didn't like the way we'd left it. We argue, but we don't end it that way. Not on edge and angry. Trying to get my mind off Ellen by thinking about Tommy wasn't especially helpful. Then there was Clare. Lovely Clare. Dangerous Clare. Ellen might just be right that people like Clare aren't worth getting hurt or killed. But I don't feel that way about Tommy. Not yet, anyway.

CHAPTER 20

A striking blond, tall and slender, walked towards me. I tried to focus my eyes. I must have fallen asleep. That's a first. She used a pair of plastic tongs to hand me a hot towel.

"Thank you. Any chance for coffee?"

"We'll be serving a light breakfast shortly," she said.

I reached into my brief bag and pulled out a small English-French phrase book. I hadn't spoken French since college, but with a little brushing up, I'd be able to find my way around. I wonder if Tony Vanelli studied a phrase book on his flight over the Atlantic?

We were twenty minutes from landing and people were glued to the windows, straining for that first glimpse of Paris, when we broke through the clouds. I read more French words for visitors... "Bonsoir, Monsieur."

We landed a little after 8 A.M . I was stiff, a little cranky and anxious to get to my hotel and into a hot shower before talking to Tommy.

Getting through customs and finding my bags on the huge carousel was easier than I anticipated, considering that several overseas flights arrived at the same time. I walked outside and took a deep breath of fresh air. The sky was overcast and the temperature was in the 50's. Cabs were lined up at the curb. I got into the first one, an older blue Mercedes sedan.

"Bonjour, Monsieur," I said. "Le Grand Hotel des Balcons sur la Rive Gauche, si'l vous plait."

"Oui, Monsieur," the driver said, and off we went. The ride into the city took almost an hour. It reminded me of Chicago. Light industry, smoke stacks, houses and apartment buildings. I played tourist and enjoyed the ride. I tried to forget why I was there. The truth would come soon enough.

As we got closer to the center of the city, morning traffic clogged the streets and people crowded the sidewalks. We crossed the Seine and entered La Rive Gauche, the Left Bank. The cabby turned off Boulevard St. Michel onto Rue Racine, turned again at the Odeon Theatre and stopped. I paid the driver and picked up my bags.

The Grand Hotel des Balcons is a storefront compared to Chicago's downtown hotels. Three windows and a small doorway face the sidewalk. A round wrought-iron sign jutted out above the door, the only indication that the hotel existed at all. I walked inside and up to the front desk. The lobby was tiny by American standards.

"Bonjour, Madame," I said. "Je m'appelle, Frank Marshall. J'ai fait reserver, si'l vous plait."

"Oui, Monsieur," she said and handed me a card to fill out. When I finished, she gave me a key and an envelope. "Vous avez un message, Monsieur."

"Merci," I said and headed for my room. I dropped my bags on the floor and opened the envelope. It was from Tommy. He'd changed hotels, but he didn't name his new one. More cloak and dagger. He wanted me to meet him in the plaza at Notre Dame at noon. I looked at my watch. He obviously knew my schedule. But I had time for that shower.

Bathed and shaved, I put on khakis, a crew-neck sweater and my running shoes. My only concession to European dress was a black turtleneck. That should fool the natives.

I walked past the Odeon Theatre and took Boulevard St. Michel all the way to the river. At the Seine, I saw the towers of Notre Dame.

The plaza in front of the Cathédrale was crowded. Merchants with push carts sold food, scarves and souvenirs to tourists. An organ grinder with a live monkey played to the delight of a dozen children. Finding Tommy would not be easy. Better for him to find me. I sat on a bench near the huge doors of Notre Dame and waited.

"Hello, Frank," a voice said behind me. "Welcome to Paris, the most beautiful city in the world." Tommy took the seat next to me. He looked thin, tired. He wore baggy black slacks and an old gray jacket that could have come from a Salvation Army store. The outfit didn't make him look healthier.

"Hello, Tom. How are things?"

He shrugged his shoulders.

"You think it's okay to talk here?"

"Probably," he said. "I watched you cross the river." He paused and looked around. "Yeah, this is all right. Besides, Morgan doesn't know you're here. Yet. Once he does, he'll put a tail on you."

"That's why you switched hotels? I wouldn't expect a tail, so I'd lead Morgan straight to you?"

He nodded.

"Where are you staying now?"

"Hotel du Pantheon," he said. "It's a quarter mile from you, across Boulevard St. Michel." Tommy pulled out a well-used map of the city and showed me. He also pointed to the Hotel Meurice. "That's where Morgan and the other guy are," he said. "You know about the Meurice, Frank?"

"Nazi headquarters," I said, confidently.

"Who's the big guy with Morgan?" he asked.

I told him about Vanelli. I also told him about my run-in with Morgan and Vanelli.

"Jesus, Frank," Tommy said. "I'm sorry you got hurt. I can't imagine why Morgan'd come after you?"

"You can't?" I said, with an edge in my voice. "I gave him my word that you'd keep your hands off of Clare. Then she leaves him a note when she runs off with you. He can't find you, so he comes looking for me."

Tommy seemed surprised. "Honest, Frank," he said. "I didn't know Clare left Morgan a note."

The overnight trip and little sleep hadn't made me very tolerant of his naiveté.

"Tommy, I'm fed up with what you don't know, or what you won't do." I sat up straight on the bench and made eye contact.

"Cut the crap, will you. Tell me the whole story. Start with how—why—you got involved with her a second time."

Tommy put his hands in his lap and hung his head. He acted like a whipped puppy. "Well. . ." he began with a sob. I was tempted to grab him by the lapels, but I needed to know what he knew if I had any hope of getting him out of this mess. I kept my mouth shut, at least for the time being.

He took a breath. "Back in Chicago, I hadn't seen Clare in quite a while. Then one day she showed up at my office. She just walked in, locked the door behind her and opened her coat. I was stunned." Tommy shook his head. "Pantyhose, Frank," he said. "All she had on was pantyhose and shoes. She leaned over and brushed her boobs across my face a couple of times and kissed me. She went down on me before I knew what happened. By the time we went to see you, we..."

"Wait a minute, Tom," I said, interrupting him. "Do you mean to tell me that all she had to was to suck you off and you forgot about Morgan and how scared you were? Is that what you're telling me?"

He looked befuddled, like he couldn't imagine why I'd asked such a dumb question. "But, Frank," he said. "She's a magnificent lover."

"I know, I know, Tommy. You keep saying that. But let's get a grip here. We all have a little good sex now and then."

"Well, I don't, goddamnit," he said, annoyed. "I haven't had 'a little good sex' like you, Frank. You think I'm going to give up the only woman who always wants to make love to me? Do you?

She thinks I'm sexy. Sexy, Frank. Do you know how that makes me feel?"

I started to say something, but the tantrum continued.

"Forgive me," he said in a mocking tone. "You probably do know how it feels to be sexy." The word, "do" got the emphasis.

I forced myself to believe that I was dealing with an adult, a scholar, some said a genius, but it was difficult. I spoke softly, hoping it would help. "Tom, I still need to know how you got here, to Paris."

"She wanted my help," he said. "She had a plan all worked out." He looked down at his hands again. "It seemed so simple. We'd get phony passports, fly to Europe and disappear. We'd be lovers forever, she said." Tommy had tears in his eyes. "That's all I wanted, Frank."

"And you believed her?" I asked. He nodded. It occurred to me that if Tommy ever started thinking rationally, Clare had only to drag her boobs across his face to pull him back.

"Did Clare explain how the plan would work?"

"Sort of," Tommy said. "She got us passports and made the reservations using false names. We flew here and stayed at the Intercontinental on the Right Bank. It was a wonderful time. We made love every day." He grinned like a teenager.

"Whose idea was it to come to my office?"

"Mine, Frank" he said. "She didn't like the idea of telling you. But I worried that Morgan would blame you for part of it. I insisted we warn you."

"If she hadn't run out on you, where to next?"

"Eastern Europe. Warsaw, maybe, or Prague. Clare figured it'd be easier to hide there."

Eastern Europe. The woman continued to amaze me. Her husband wouldn't have contacts in the rubble of the Soviet client states. It was brilliant.

"Clare said we could live better in Eastern Europe. Of course, we had plenty of money to live anywhere we liked, really. I wanted to stay in Paris."

"Where'd you get the money?" I asked. "Was it hers?"

"Actually, it's Morgan's money. Clare stole it."

"She what?" I couldn't believe what I'd just heard.

"Uh, huh," he said. "She took one million dollars in thousand dollar bills. A thousand of 'em, to be exact. If we invested right, we could live well for a long time. But... it didn't quite work out that way."

"You guys are fuckin' nuts," I said. "You know that? Taking a million of Morgan's dollars. It's not bad enough that he wants his wife back, or your ass on a platter—now you've got his cash, too. How dumb can you be? No wonder he high-tailed it over here."

A long line of tourists waited at a small door to get into Notre Dame. They seemed very excited. "Come on," I said. "Let's go for a walk."

We headed off along the river, next to the Cathédrale. The sun was out and it felt warm despite the chilly fall air. We stopped at a railing overlooking the Seine, near the French memorial to Holocaust survivors.

"Is Clare still in the city?"

"Why? What difference does that make?"

"Listen, Tom," I said. "You want me to get you out of this business with Morgan, right?"

He nodded.

"Well, if I'm going to save your ass, giving him his money back might help."

"She'll never give the money back, Frank. It's her lifeline."

"Leave that to me," I said. It sounded like I had a plan. I didn't. "Where is she?"

"A hotel near the Eiffel Tower. Here, I'll show you." Tommy took out his map again. He pointed out the Eiffel Tower, the Ecole Militaire down the street. "There," he said, pointing. "Saxe Residence Hotel. That's where she is. Margaret Harvey is the phony name."

We stood, silent, for a few minutes and watched the river. A tourist boat, a *baton mouche*, cruised by filled with tourists. A voice on a loudspeaker described something on shore.

"Frank," Tommy said softly, "what am I going to do?"

"With some luck, Tom, I'll get you out of this. But it's the last time. I'm all through feeling guilty about our childhood, about Pop and the beatings. I'll save you from getting hurt this time, but that's it."

"That's not what I mean." He hesitated. "What am I going to do without Clare? I can't live without her." He was crying. I felt badly for him, but not that bad.

"Tom, there are other woman in the world, if that's what you want," I said. Sooner or later you have to face the fact that Clare took you for a ride." He had a disgusted look on his face. "Her only motive, her only objective, as near as I can tell, is to get away from her husband. Period. She'll use anybody to make that happen. Including you."

Tommy sobbed openly. "But she knows what I want, Frank. She makes me happy. What'll I do without her?"

"Damn it, Tom. You could start by taking some responsibility for what you do. Your dick has gotten a lot of people in trouble, especially you. And here I am trying to bail you out again because I feel guilty. One of these days, there won't be anyone to do that. Not even me."

He nodded his head, but I could tell he really didn't comprehend what I meant. Maybe he never would.

"I'm tired, Tommy," I said. "Tired and hungry. I'll call you in the morning after I've had time to think about things."

He nodded his head and walked away without saying goodbye.

I needed to clear my head. I looked at the Seine for a few minutes, then walked down the stairs to the Holocaust Memorial. I wanted to be a tourist for a while.

CHAPTER 21

I rolled over in bed and looked at my watch. It read 8.33. I sat up on edge of the bed and opened the drapes. The sky was blue. People moved quickly on the sidewalk. They wore coats and I could see steam coming out of their mouths.

I took a shower, shaved and put on the same clothes from the night before. I walked downstairs and into the small dining room. It was a plain room with a marble floor like the lobby but no windows. People who looked more like business people than tourists occupied most of the tables. I sat down at an empty two-top in the corner.

"Bonjour, Monsieur," the waitress said.

"Bonjour," I said. "Café noir, si'l vous plait." I opened a map of the city. I found my hotel, the Seine, the Eiffel Tower and Clare's hotel near Avenue de Saxe. The waitress brought croissants, jam and black coffee. The coffee was strong.

I thought about how to contact Clare. If I called her on the phone, she'd have time to run. I won't find her in Eastern Europe. Better to catch her face-to-face. Then I'd convince her to give back the money, charming devil that I am. If that didn't work, I could always do, well, something else. Didn't know what that might be.

I looked at the map and traced a route to Clare's hotel. It was only about three miles. No point in taking a cab or the Metro on a nice fall day. I'd rather walk. I finished my coffee, signed the check, and left my key at the desk.

The sun had warmed the air. I started off, map in hand, towards the river. The narrow streets of the Left Bank were lined with small shops, restaurants, even a theater that ran Alfred Hitchcock films fourteen hours a day. More reminders of Chicago's North Side. I turned at the Seine and walked west.

No, I still hadn't figured out what exactly to say to Clare. Maybe she'd give Morgan the money if I could convince him to let her go. That assumed a lot of brilliant moves on my part.

The route took almost an hour. I saw the Eiffel Tower in the distance. I stopped and stared just like a tourist. I continued walking up the Champ de Mars, an open grassy area between the Eiffel Tower and the École Militaire. On the other side of the military school, I spotted the sign for Clare's hotel on a block-long cul-de-sac off the main street. I had to find out if she was still registered.

I walked up the short street and into the lobby. It was very small. Behind the desk sat an officious looking man in his late fifties wearing a gray pinstriped suit and horn rimmed glasses.

"Bonjour, Monsieur," I said.

He greeted me with an arrogant shrug.

I asked if Margaret Harvey—the name Tommy gave me—was in.

The man turned on his stool and reached for the slotted box on the wall behind him. He felt slot 3-A.

"Non, Monsieur."

"Merci," I said and left him to whatever I'd interrupted, but I now knew Clare's room number. Unfortunately the stairs and elevator were across from Monsieur Friendly's desk.

I walked back outside and took up residence on a bench on the sidewalk near the cul-de-sac. I waited.

In less than an hour, I spotted her coming down the street. She wore a navy two-piece jogging suit. Her blond hair was tied into a ponytail with a bright red ribbon, and she carried a baguette of bread under her arm. I crossed the street and walked towards her. She saw me, slowed her pace, then stopped.

"Why, Mr. Marshall," she said coyly, "what a delightful surprise."

I reached out and we shook hands. "How are you, Ms. Morgan," I said, "or is it 'Harvey'?"

She smiled. "I see you've been talking to Tom."

"Aren't you making it easier for your husband to find you by walking around in the open?"

"No," she said emphatically. "Ricky wouldn't lower himself to visit La Rive Gauche. He wouldn't want anyone to think he couldn't afford La Rive Droite or the Hotel Meurice. Do you know about the Meurice, Mr. Marshall?"

"Nazi headquarters," I said firmly. When would people stop asking that question?

"Fitting, is it not?" she said with a grin. "Would you like a piece of bread?" Clare pulled back the white paper and tore off the end of the baguette for herself. I helped myself to a two-inch piece.

"Do you mind if I call you Clare?" I asked.

"Not if I can call you Frank."

"Please do. Clare, I need your help. Is there someplace we can talk?"

"I figured you weren't in Paris to see the sights," she said. "Why don't we sit up by La Tour Eiffel. It's such a lovely spot, and there are enough people around that I'll feel safe. No, offense, Frank."

"None taken."

We walked up the Champ de Mars and found a bench in the trees, a few hundred feet from the tower.

Clare tore another chunk of bread from the loaf. "Now, Frank, why do you need my help?"

"Tommy Marshall," I said, and waited.

She nodded her head and looked up at the iron structure, then back at me.

"I know," she sighed, "I know. I didn't mean to hurt him. I really like Tom, at least most of the time. When he turns into that pitiful child," she shook her head, "he's not very likable." It seemed like an honest answer, but trusting Clare wouldn't be easy.

"You hurt him bad," I said. "And more than once."

Clare stiffened. "Is this going to be a lecture?" she asked sharply. "I don't need a lecture from you or anyone else. If you want my help, get on with it. Otherwise, I'll be on my way."

"I'm trying to save Tommy's head," I said. "Your husband wants it on a platter. And you're responsible." That wasn't entirely true, but I wanted to see how she'd respond.

"Partly responsible," she said. "Tommy's an adult. He makes his own decisions. Let him suffer the consequences."

"He's only an adult some of the time," I said. "And right now he's a mess because you walked out on him and because your husband wants to cut his balls off."

Clare started to say something, then stopped.

"Maybe he'll be a love-sick puppy for the rest of his life. But I want to keep him alive and get your husband off his back. Now, will you help?"

Clare handed me the bread. I tore off another piece and took a bite.

"I'm listening," she said, but she wasn't too happy about it.

"First of all, I want to clear up a couple of things. Did you plan this getaway before or after you met Tommy?"

"Neither one, actually. I've been trying to figure out how to get away from my husband for a long time. Some of the details, like the passports, were easy. Putting it all together was the problem. Ricky has lots of contacts. Bad guys who'll do anything for money."

"You needed a sucker who'd fall for you?"

"Frank," she said, leaning forward on the bench, "you may not believe me, but I liked Tom when we met. I was attracted to him. He's charming, light-hearted and smart. He's everything Ricky'll never be. It wasn't 'till after Ricky'd found us out that I thought Tom might be, well, useful to me. I knew my husband would be obsessed with any man I got involved with. I figured I could use that."

Tommy had chased her repeatedly, Clare said, to re-ignite the affair even though I'd settled things with Morgan.

"He'd follow me, show up in parking lots, supermarkets and restaurants. He didn't tell it to you that way, did he?"

I shook my head.

"He acted like, well, like a puppy. That's when I thought I might persuade him to help me out."

"Persuade? Don't you mean you offered sex as a reward?"

"How dare you moralize to me," she said angrily. "You don't know the hell I lived, so don't be so quick to judge what I'd do to get out. Anyone's better than my husband, and anything's better than sex with him. He fancies himself as god's gift, but he's an oaf. His idea of satisfying a woman is how fast he can slam it in before he comes. Doesn't that sound like fun? If I complained, or asked him to be gentle, he'd tell me to shut up. Or at least he used to." She looked at the ground. "Now he hits me. I've had enough, that's all."

"How long has that been going on?" I asked.

She shrugged her shoulders. "Four or five years." Her face reddened, as if it embarrassed her to admit she'd let it go on that long. "It felt nice that Tom liked to make love to me. A little good sex never hurt anyone."

The woman's life is on a string and she flirts.

"You need to understand something, Mr. Marshall," she said, emphasizing the return to formality. "Nobody just walks away from Rick Morgan. Don't you know that? Nobody. Especially his wife. He wouldn't let me challenge his power that way. His ego couldn't take it. I'd use anyone, I'd use sex, I'd use whatever it takes."

"But you set Tom Marshall up to take the fall, and it might get him killed," I said. "Isn't that carrying things too far?"

Clare bolted off the bench, turned towards me, hands on her hips. "Let me be clear. I used Tom. Hell, I even used you."

My face must have reacted.

"Yes, you, Frank."

We were back to a first-name basis.

"Once Tom got you into this, it was easy. If Tom was in big trouble, I knew you'd be along sooner or later to get him out of it." She sat back down on the bench. "I know all about your family. What it was like at home. You were suckered by his helplessness. I took advantage of that. We came to your office that day so Tom could warn you, but I knew that it would buy us time. My husband would go after you first when he couldn't find us."

I could see Ellen's I-told-you-so look now.

"You were a necessary diversion," she said. "Hell, you're a diversion now. As soon as Rick finds out you're in Paris, he'll come after you. And he'll find Tom eventually. Don't you see, he has to tie up the loose ends? Tom was my lover and you humiliated him into backing down. He has to take care of both of you. And while he's chasing you two, I'll be on my way."

"He'll come after Tom and me, sure," I said, "but you overlooked one thing."

"And that is?" she said with confidence that nothing had been missed.

"The money. He's gonna want the million back."

Clare froze in place, like I'd slapped her. It didn't take her long to recover.

"Bullshit," she said. "If you think I'm giving him that money, you're sadly mistaken. I need it to get away, to live on."

"Maybe I'll have to trade you and the money for my brother."

She looked at me with angry eyes. "You wouldn't do that, Frank," she said. "You're not that kind of man. But if you try that, I'll be out of this town before you get to his hotel."

"Maybe. Or maybe your plans aren't working so well, or you'd be in Warsaw or Prague right now."

"I see Tom told you what I had in mind," she said. "It's still a good plan. I just need a little time, that's all." Clare looked right at me. "You wouldn't necessarily have to tell my husband right away, would you?" she asked coyly, as she slowly dragged the index finger of her right hand down from her throat, between her breasts, to her waist and stopped. Clare seemed to shift back and forth from a desperate woman trying to save herself and an actress in a steamy thriller.

"Is that all you know how to do?" I asked. "Seduce men?"

She didn't miss a beat. "I do it very well, you know."

"So I've heard."

"Very, very well." She unzipped her jacket and pulled it open with her fingers. She wore nothing but cleavage.

"Clare, you're a beautiful woman. But seducing me won't get you anywhere. Start trusting your brain for a change. If you really want to get away from your husband, you've got to help me."

Her face looked sad, and she zipped up the jacket.

"Rick's going to come after you eventually," I said, "especially if you still have his money. You'll never be free unless he doesn't want you any more. You'll spend the rest of your life looking over your shoulder. Paris, Prague, Chicago. It doesn't matter."

"I know that." For the first time since all this started, Clare Morgan seemed vulnerable.

"Suppose I told you that I have a plan to save Tommy's neck and yours at the same time."

She looked at me intently.

"Interested?"

She nodded. "What makes you think my husband would let any of us go?"

"Because I'll convince him it's in his best interest to do so," I said.

Clare had a skeptical look on her face, and I didn't blame her. I would sound more convincing if I actually had a plan.

"How's this supposed to work?" she asked.

"I'm still pulling the details together. I'll get back to you in a day or two, okay?"

We walked back down the Champ de Mars, towards Clare's hotel.

"Are you going to tell my husband you found me?"

"Not as long as you stick around for a few days so I can lay out the details," I said.

Clare didn't say anything, but she put her arm through mine as we walked. I wrote the name of my hotel on the back of a business card and gave it to her when we got to her hotel.

"Call if you need me."

"You don't have to go right now, do you, Frank?" she asked. Clare put her arms around my waist and pulled me close.

"Yeah, I do," I said. I put my arms around Clare and gave her a hug. "I'll get you out of this, Clare."

"That's not why I put my arms around you."

"I know that. I'll make this work."

"I hope so, Frank."

We said good-bye and I got out my map and found Napoleon's Tomb. Maybe the Emperor would inspire me to devise a clever plan. I sure needed one.

CHAPTER 22

I sat at a window table in the Café de Cluny. I ordered a café au lait and watched cars and people crowd together outside. They meshed more easily than they do in Chicago. I wondered why.

I liked watching the Parisian world go by, but it wasn't helping me create a plan.

So far I'd talked with Tommy, but he was too caught up in his own misery to be of any help. Clare was more honest and more willing to listen despite her reluctance to accept help. But she was desperate to be rid of Morgan. The only one I hadn't talked to was Morgan himself. I didn't like the idea of telling him I was in Paris, but he'd find out soon enough. Like Clare, he'd have figured I'd show up to help Tommy.

Like it or not, I had to call Morgan. He was the one hunting Clare and Tommy. He was the only one who could put an end to it.

I finished my café au lait, walked to Rue Racine and turned right.

The desk clerk at the Balcons handed me a telephone message when I picked up my room key. Jacque wanted me to call. The six-hour time difference left me a few hours before she went home. Back in my room, I first looked up Hotel Meurice in the phone book, dialed the number and asked for Morgan.

"Hello," Tony Vanelli said. "Who's-a dis?"

"Dis-a Frank Marshall," I said. "Put your boss on." Vanelli must have covered the mouthpiece because I heard soft, muffled talking. Then Morgan came on the line.

"Hi ya, punk," he said in a flat voice. "Figured I hear from you."

"Glad to see you're picking up a little culture," I said. "Traveling's good for the soul."

"Fuck you, Marshall."

"Ah, it's comforting to know that some things never change."

"You gonna play funny man or tell me why you called?"

"I want to talk," I said. "Tonight. In a public place with lots of people."

"You coming alone?"

I said yes.

"That's too bad," Morgan said. "I was looking forward to renewing my acquaintance with the professor."

"Now who's being funny?"

We agreed to meet in the lobby of the Hotel Meurice. It was as safe as I could get. Even with Vanelli there, Morgan wouldn't try any strong-arm stuff. It'd ruin his image as a classy guy from America.

I looked up the country code for the States and phoned Jacque. Winkler, Norton and Barger continued in business despite my absence. My cases were still on hold. Except for one.

"Denise Kirshner's in Paris," Jacque said. "She got dumped by her boyfriend a few days ago and Mr. Winkler wants you to call her. She's all alone."

"Did she call Winkler to cry on his shoulder?" I asked.

"Hardly. Allison DeWolf told me Mr. Winkler sent her some papers by overnight courier. Something's brewing at DCN Manufacturing."

"Am I supposed to baby-sit her?"

"Don't be so cynical, Frank," Jacque said. "She's Mr. Winkler's friend, and a good client, and her man ran out on her. She's there, you're there. You know..." Jacque gave me the hotel name and phone number.

"How are you doing, by the way?"

"I'm all right." I gave her a recap of events since I arrived in Paris. "But my patience is wearing thin with all of them, including my brother. I'd rather be back in the office, digging into somebody's background. These are not nice people, Jacque, and it could rub off."

I hung up and called the Hotel Crillon and asked for Denise Kirshner. She answered on the second ring.

"Bonjour, Madame Kirshner," I said. "This is Frank Marshall."

"Why, Mr. Marshall, what a surprise."

I explained why I called. She appreciated the gesture.

"How about dinner tomorrow night?" I asked. "You pick the restaurant since you know the city so well."

"Good idea. I'd like to see a familiar face. Where are you staying?"

I told her. "It's near the Odeon Theatre."

"Then let's go to Le Polidor. It's the best restaurant in the city."

"It's a deal," I said, "where is it?"

"It's a block from the Theatre." She gave me directions. "I'll meet you there at eight."

I called Tommy at his hotel, but he was out. I left a message. Then I tried Clare. She wasn't happy that her husband knew that I was in Paris. I explained that unless I talked to Morgan face-to-face, I had no chance to work things out for her or Tommy. I told her I'd call again in the morning.

I took the Metro from the Odeon stop to Chatelet and changed trains. I got off at Tuileries and came above ground on the Rue de Rivoli. The Hotel Meurice took up the whole block across the street. The doorman tipped his hat as I walked by him. I nodded.

The lobby was as spacious as mine was small. Wood paneling, large plants and small groups of couches, chairs and tables gave the lobby an intimate feel despite its size. I looked around for Morgan. Then I saw Tony Vanelli. He was dressed all in black, but it didn't conceal his size. He was an imposing man.

"Wait-a here," he said. "I got-a call Mr. Morgan."

I nodded.

Vanelli went to a small desk and picked up a house phone. I waited by the large window next to the front door. Lamps in the Tuileries across the street gave off a soft glow. A young couple walked side-by-side holding hands, laughing. Lincoln Park and Ellen seemed very far away.

"Mr. Morgan will-a be here soon," Vanelli said. "You talk over there." He pointed to a parlor off the main lobby. It was a miniature version of the lobby, but without windows. A few chairs, a couch and a coffee table were clustered around a fireplace. I took off my jacket and picked an overstuffed chair so I could see the lobby through the doorway.

Five minutes later, Rick Morgan arrived wearing a brown suit, brown shoes and green and brown tie. Natty. Where are the fashion police when you need them?

"Hello, Marshall. What are you drinking?" Morgan pointed at the waiter who followed him into the room.

"Café noir, sil vous plait," I said.

The waiter nodded.

"Think you're pretty fancy, don't you," Morgan said. "Give me a tonic with a twist. A lemon twist this time." The waiter turned and left. Morgan looked at Vanelli. "You check him?" Vanelli shook his head.

"Too many people, boss." Vanelli was classier than his boss.

"I have no gun," I said.

Morgan waved his hand in my direction and I stood up while Vanelli frisked me. I saw a shoulder holster under Vanelli's blazer.

"How the hell did you get a weapon into the country?"

"We do what we need to do," Morgan said, smiling. Perhaps he was more connected than I'd given him credit for. The waiter brought our drinks, and Morgan signed the tab. He sat in the chair across from me. Vanelli took up residence on the other side of the room, near the door. Morgan sipped his tonic and smacked his lips. Now I was sure that Vanelli was classier than his boss.

Morgan looked at me and said, "You called this meeting."

"We've got to put an end to all of this," I said, waving my arm in the air.

"Don't worry, I'll put an end to it. Count on it." He sounded too calm, like he was buying a car. I didn't like that.

"We've had our differences..."

"You can bet your ass on that."

"...but this has gone on too long. You and I have to find a way to stop it before somebody gets hurt."

"Not somebody," Morgan said. "The professor. He's the one I'm gonna hurt. Then you." He picked up his tonic and took a drink. He glanced at Vanelli who stood, arms folded, staring at the floor. "I want to tell you about Professor Thomas Marshall. See, I do know his name. But I don't like to say the name of the asshole who's fucking my wife. I'll never let her go to another man. You understand? Tony's gonna kill him." Vanelli looked up at the mention of his name. "But first I'm gonna cut his dick off and hand it to him."

Morgan turned towards Vanelli and snapped his fingers. Vanelli unfolded his arms and reached into his jacket pocket. Out came a long switchblade. He pushed a button and the six-inch blade cracked to life. Probably the knife he used to cut Ronnie Birch. No wonder the poor guy was so scared.

Morgan meant what he said. He obviously hadn't come to Paris for the museums. I wasn't sure that I could convince him to let Tommy live, but I had to try.

"You won't gain a thing by killing my brother."

Morgan smiled and pointed his index finger at me. "Satisfaction," he said. "And he'll never fuck my wife again."

"I'll keep him away from Clare."

"What do you take me for, Marshall?" he said, his voice louder. He was angry. "You gave me your word before, you sonofabitch. I had you checked out. Did you know that?"

I didn't know.

"My people said you were okay. A little stubborn but a straight shooter. So I believed you. Give me a reason... any reason... I shouldn't hurt both of you."

"Because I know things you need to know," I said.

"Such as?"

"Such as your wife is through with Tom Marshall," I said.

The mere mention of Clare caught Morgan off guard. "How do you know that?"

"Because I talked to her."

That surprised him, too.

"It was Clare who started the affair again. She's the one who got Tommy back in it."

Morgan was hot now. He could barley contain himself. It's a good thing plenty of people crowded the lobby next door.

"You fuck!" he said in a shouted whisper. "You've got balls blaming my wife for your brother's wandering dick. You got nerve!"

"Your wife doesn't give a shit about Marshall. This isn't about sex."

That caught him. "But you just said..."

"Morgan, listen to me. Clare doesn't give a damn about Tommy Marshall, or any other man for that matter. She wants out. It's that simple. She cooked up a plan to get away from you.

Marshall was part of that plan, that's all. She just wants to go away alone."

"You bastard! You goddamn bastard! Who the hell do you think you are? Come here and tell me my wife wants to get rid of me." Morgan got out of his chair and took a step my way. I shot a quick glance at Vanelli who was suddenly very interested in what his boss was doing. "I outta let Tony kill you right here. Right now."

"Go ahead," I said, trying to sound confident. "Go ahead and see how many people push their way in here to see what happened. Both of you'll be in jail before midnight."

That stopped him for the moment.

"I talked to Clare this morning and she told me the whole story. She said..." I stopped talking. Morgan was stunned. Vanelli, too.

"You don't know where she is, do you?" I said. "You haven't found her yet."

Morgan backed up a step. He picked up his glass and drank some tonic. "Where is she?" he demanded.

"Well..." I let my voice trail off. I hadn't touched my coffee. Now seemed like a good time. It was cold.

"I could force you to talk, you sonofabitch," he said. "And not here either. Where there'd be no witnesses."

"You could do that, all right. But if Vanelli works me over, Clare'll be on the first train out of here and you'll never get your million bucks back."

That one put him right back in his chair, speechless. Almost.

"How'd you find out about the money?"

"How doesn't matter. You want your money back?"

"The money... and my wife," Morgan said, emphatically.

"You want the money, I can help," I said. "But not Clare. She gets what she wants."

"The money and Clare," Morgan repeated, each word spoken slowly and deliberately.

So far, so good. This might be a good time to push.

"I can get you the money. The price is Clare. Right now, you don't have either one. Think about it."

"Bullshit," Morgan said. "Think about this. Tony picks up the professor and we have a little party. Just the four of us. You get dead. He tells me where Clare is before I ram his cock down his throat."

"Bullshit," I said. "You don't know where Tommy is either, or you'd have him already."

Morgan never took his eyes off me, but he said, "Tony."

"Hotel next to the Pantheon, room 403." Clare was right. Morgan hoped to follow the lovesick puppy straight to her.

"Why don't you tell me where my wife is and save us all a lot of trouble?"

"No," I said, "not yet, anyway. If we work out a deal, I'll get you the money..."

"No deals!" Morgan said. "I'm through talking. I find Clare. I get the money, the professor gets dead and we all live happily ever after." He laughed, then Vanelli laughed.

I didn't feel like laughing. The money was the only card I had to play. If Clare ran off before I convinced her to give it back, things would get ugly in a hurry.

"What I want to know," I said, not very confident about my skill at bluffing. "Do you want the money or don't you?"

"I always listen when someone talks money," Morgan said.

I couldn't tell if he meant it or not. I had nothing to lose pretending that he did.

"In that case," I said, "I'll be in touch." I stood and picked up my jacket. Morgan and Vanelli got up, too. I moved towards the door. Morgan reached out and grabbed my arm as I walked by him. He held it firmly enough to stop me.

"Tell me where Clare is," he said. "I'll settle my business with the professor and you can be on the next plane to Chicago. Keep getting in my way..." he shrugged his shoulders. "You know what will happen."

I lifted Morgan's hand off my arm and left the parlor. Neither of them followed me. I crossed the street against traffic. I stopped at the top of the Metro stairway and looked back at the Hotel Meurice. Majestic, elegant and fifty years ago, Nazi headquarters.

Thirty minutes later, I sat on the front steps of the Odeon Theatre and added up the promises I'd made since landing in Paris. It was a long list and growing longer. I'd promised Tommy I'd save his ass if not his love life. I told Clare I'd convince Morgan to let her go, and I told Morgan I'd get his money back. I didn't have a clue how to do any of them.

CHAPTER 23

In the morning, I walked to the Odeon newsstand and bought *USA Today* and the *International Herald Tribune*. I missed Chicago and I missed Ellen. I went back and ate breakfast in the hotel dining room again. The United States seemed to be chugging away like always.

After finishing a third cup of coffee, I wrote my number on the check and went to my room to call Clare. At least I'd keep one promise.

She was cranky when she came on the line. It was 10.30. I endured several minutes of slurs and idle chitchat before she was alert enough to listen. I lied and told her that the meeting with her husband went well.

"Clare," I said, "if I find a way for you to get free of your husband in exchange for the money, will you do it?"

"No."

"Would you consider it?"

"Depends."

Ah, progress. She wanted to know what I had in mind. I had nothing in mind, so I said that I was working on it and she bought it, which bought me some time.

I called Tommy. He was out, so I left a message.

I had no idea how I was going to keep all the plates spinning, but something would come to me.

Tommy hadn't returned my calls when I left to have dinner with Denise Kirshner. I wore a navy blazer over a burgundy crew-neck and of course, another pair of khakis. Chicago dressy. The night was cool and clear. Cars were parked everywhere—in the usual places and in some innovative spots that never would have occurred to hardened veterans of the Windy City.

Restaurant Le Polidor, on Monsieur-le-Prince, was only a block up from my hotel, looking much like it must have in the 1920s when Hemingway and Joyce were regulars. Long rectangular tables jutted out from the sidewalls. A waitress in her twenties, dressed in a white blouse and long black skirt, sat me near the end of one of the tables. I faced the door. Before the waitress could put a basket of bread on the table, Denise Kirshner walked in. I waved and she saw me.

We'd only met twice, but her grace and elegance were evident as she walked to the table. Her navy wool suit was sporty rather than business, and she carried a tan Coach shoulder bag. I stood and extended my hand.

"Good evening, Ms. Kirshner."

"Good evening, Mr. Marshall," she said, shaking my hand. "How does Frank and Denise sound?"

"It sounds fine." Her black hair was almost to her shoulders now. It had gained lots of soft curls as it grew longer. A simple gold frog was pinned to the lapel of her jacket.

"Bonsoir, Madame et Monsieur," the waitress said, handing each of us a menu.

"Bonsoir," I said. "Vin blanc du maison, si'l vous plait." I looked at Denise who agreed with a nod.

"It was nice of you to call, Frank. Paris is a lovely city, but it feels too big right now."

"It's a pleasure, Denise. Besides, it's fun to have dinner with someone I know so far from home."

"Didn't you tell me you had friends in Paris? Did I misunderstand?"

I shook my head. I described what I was doing, without the messy details. I focused on the dead romance aspects of Tommy and Clare and left out the rest. Denise nodded knowingly as I talked of lost love.

"Yes," she said, "I've had my fill of that sort of thing for a while. Not that it wasn't fun. Jason and I had a wonderful time."

The waitress brought a carafe of white wine and poured some for us. I raised my glass in Denise's direction. She touched my glass with hers.

"What happened?" I asked. "If I'm not intruding."

"You're not intruding, Frank. After all, you and Harold warned me that this would happen. But you're not going to say, 'I told you so' are you?"

I shook my head. "I don't live that way."

"Somehow, I didn't think so." With that, Denise launched into a long but interesting recap of her romantic travels with the recently departed Jason Donaldson. They played the role of wealthy American tourists at every opportunity, living and eating well along the way. "We had a glorious time," she said. There was a sparkle in her eyes as she shared fond memories.

The waitress took our order. I picked Boeuf Bourguignon and Denise the lamb and green beans.

"Have you ever been to Berlin?" she asked.

I shook my head.

"Neither had I. But I wanted to see where the wall used to be. I wanted to stand there. I'm older than you, Frank. I remember the fear of the Soviets. I never thought I'd live to see the wall come down."

Denise Kirshner had the spirit of a teenager and a spark to her life that belied her age. Most people her age did little more than give the front-porch swing a good workout.

"Jason and I were in London for a few days when he started to get phone calls. He got secretive about it. I wasn't, you should pardon the expression, born yesterday," she said, grinning. "I confronted him about the calls." She poured more wine for both of us. I took another piece of bread. "It was an old flame from the States. Apparently her family has houses in Marseilles and Rome. She'd tracked him down. I told him to pack his bags and get out. He did."

The waitress set two plates of steaming food on the table. I ordered more wine, and it arrived at the table accompanied by another basket of bread.

"Denise, If you knew this would happen, why get tangled up with him?"

I told you before, Frank. My late husband was a genius at humiliating me. Jason made me feel wanted, desirable. He is... was a spectacular lover who knew all the right things to say to make me feel wonderful. But he was too dumb to figure out that I still controlled the money." Denise looked away for a minute. "I had to get something out of my system. I needed one man, a good-looking one to boot, to tear my clothes off at every opportunity. I needed to feel that."

"I don't understand something," I said. "You're a self-made woman. Bright, attractive, successful. Why did you need an empty-headed stud to make you feel better?"

"Because I'm human," she said. "Because I'm not always as confident as I appear to be."

"I admire your honesty."

She smiled and tipped her wine glass in my direction. I picked up my glass and returned the gesture. "So what are your plans now?" I asked.

"DCN Manufacturing," she said without hesitation. "I'm taking control of the company. Everything's in the works. As soon as I get word from Harold, I'll fly to Chicago."

I thought back to what Jacque said on the phone. "Anything to do with the papers sent by courier?"

"You are a good investigator."

"Thanks for the compliment," I said, "but I can't take the credit. My secretary called me."

Denise laughed. "I've already sent the papers back, by the way. My daughter signed over her 15% of the stock to me and returned the 20% I signed over to her a while ago. That'll give me 55% of the company's stock and absolute control."

"I thought she'd sided with her brothers."

"Elizabeth, bless her heart, wanted what was best for the company. When Jason came into my life, she thought I'd gone off the deep end. She believed Kyle and Charles, Jr. were more capable of running the company."

"Why the change of heart, then?"

"She found out that her brothers had dollar signs instead of hearts. They want to sell DCN to a holding company in Seattle. They only want money. Elizabeth was furious. She tried to reason with them, to no avail. She contacted Harold who contacted me. As for Kyle and Charles? Fuck 'em," Denise said without anger. It was all business. "I downsized DCN and made it a more viable business than at any time since my husband founded it. It's a good company, and I won't let it go because Charles and Kyle want new Porsches every year."

The waitress cleared the table of empty dishes. She looked at us expectantly.

I said, "Café noir, si'l vous plait."

"Moi, aussi," Denise added. "Besides, Frank, life's a little dull these days. I don't need another Jason in my life. I got that out of my system. Next time, I'll find a man who appreciates me for who I am."

Our coffee arrived. Mine tasted strong and rich.

"That's more than you wanted to hear about my life. How about you? Tell me about Frank Marshall."

I did. About my work, about Ellen, and more about Tommy.

"Your brother sounds very unhappy," she said. "Not because of the woman. Just unhappy."

"I'm beginning to think so, too. I thought I knew my brother pretty well before all this started. It isn't that he's got a dark side. We all have a shadow lurking someplace. It's his recklessness. He causes damage that other people have to clean up. He only thinks about what affects him."

The waitress put the check on the table and I picked it up, looked it over.

"Something wrong?" Denise asked.

"On the contrary," I said. "That was a wonderful meal at sandwich prices."

"I'm glad you enjoyed it," she said. "Shall we walk?"

We left Le Polidor and walked up the street, towards the Odeon Theatre.

"I'm heading to the Odeon Metro stop. I'll walk you to your hotel," Denise said. "I certainly had a pleasant evening. I hope we have an opportunity to meet again."

"Good idea," I said. "I'll pick a Chicago restaurant."

"It's a deal. That would give me a chance to meet Ellen. She sounds like a wonderful woman, and she's quite lucky to have you."

I thanked her for the compliment and we said good night.

The night clerk handed me a message with my room key. Tommy had finally returned my calls. I went upstairs and called his hotel, but he was out, again. I had to leave another message.

I must have dozed off reading the newspapers because I was lying on the bed fully dressed when the phone rang. I struggled to pick it up and muttered a greeting.

"Marshall?" a voice said. It sounded familiar, but I was groggy.

"Yeah. Who's this?"

"Hold on," the voice said. Another voice came on the line. I had no trouble identifying the new voice.

"Hi ya, punk," Rick Morgan said in his usual warm and friendly manner. "Catching a few ZZZs, are you?" I looked at my watch. It read 5:40.

"How'd you know where to find me?"

"Shit. You punks are all alike," he said. The manner was condescending. "I know what I know, asshole. The rest I find out."

"So what do you want? I want to go back to sleep."

"Fuck you. I'll let you know when I'm done with you."

"I'm listening."

"I got your brother, punk," he said. I sat up on the bed. The adrenalin hit hard.

"Is he all right?"

"He's just fine. For now. Oh, he's nursing a sore jaw. The professor thought he was tough enough to take Tony." Morgan laughed. "He wasn't." I heard someone else laughing.

"I want to talk to him, Morgan," I said. "Right now."

"I call the shots, asshole," Morgan said, angrily. "We got business to do, you and me, so..."

"Put him on the phone or I don't do business." I heard shuffling, noise on the line.

"Frank?" It was Tommy.

"You okay, Tommy?" I asked.

"Yeah," he said.

That was all he said. Morgan came back on the line.

"Here's how it's gonna be, Marshall," he said, calmer now. "I got the professor here and I want to make a trade, nice fella that

I am." He chuckled. "I'll give him to you. And I want my wife and the money, the whole million."

It was clear that Morgan still hadn't found Clare or we wouldn't be playing this little game.

"So what do you want from me," I said, trying to play dumb.

"Cut the bullshit, punk. Get Clare, get the money and bring them to me."

"And if I don't?"

"If you don't, the Paris cops are going to find your brother in the river."

"What makes you thing Clare will listen to me?"

"I don't give a fat fuck if she listens to you or not," he said. "Get her and the money. I'm through talking."

"What if I can't find her?" I said. "What if she's left town already?" No quick response this time. Maybe he hadn't thought of that.

"Then you find her, punk. You got twenty-four hours." I heard a click and the line went dead.

I put the phone down. If Clare gets wind of this and runs, I'll never find her in time to save Tommy. If Morgan has to search for her, Tommy's a dead man.

CHAPTER 24

The street sweepers seemed louder than usual this morning. I sat on the side of the bed, rubbed my face with my hands, then pulled back the drapes. The darkness had begun to lift, the sky was clear.

I'd love to really be a tourist today and run in Jardin du Luxembourg. The emotional strain of the last few days had taken its toll. Running restores some balance to my life, but nothing will do much good if Morgan kills Tommy.

I needed to think this through logically before I called Clare.

Which was a curious notion since this entire saga was anything but logical.

I went into the bathroom and splashed cold water on my face. I put on khakis, a sweater and went downstairs to get some coffee. The waitress served me black coffee and rolls.

Morgan said he would trade Tommy for Clare and the money. Would he trade only for the money? Doubtful.

I sipped the strong coffee.

I could appeal to his finer instincts, but I'm not sure he has finer instincts. He does have Tony Vanelli, which doesn't make things any finer.

Tommy, on the other hand, doesn't have a choice. If he wants to live, he's got to quit Clare once and for all. Getting kidnapped by Morgan and Vanelli might scare him into that.

Would Clare give up the money if Morgan let her go?

The waitress poured more coffee and put a magazine on my table. The cover featured the miniature replica of the Statue of Liberty in the Luxembourg Gardens. I wished I were running by it right now.

The money is the key. If Clare keeps it, she'll have to run, and Tommy's dead. If Morgan gets his money back, he might, just might, let Clare go if I could convince him it was in his interest to do so. But Clare won't return the money without an alternate plan that guarantees her safety and enough money to live.

I looked down at the magazine cover again. For some reason, I remembered the old Statue of Liberty play in football. The defense watches the quarterback. The defense thinks he is about to pass, when the running back grabs the ball and is gone. The play is about trickery and diversion. I could use a little of both right now. A good running back is like an alternate plan. I need someone to take the ball.

All of a sudden I had it. A plan and a running back. Could it work? What did I have to lose? I signed the check, left a franc on the table and ran upstairs to call the Hotel Carillon.

"Why, Frank," Denise Kirshner said, "so nice to hear from you."

"Good morning, Denise. Can I meet you some place? I'd like to talk about something important."

"Sounds exciting."

"It's more business than pleasure, I'm afraid. Although it's not Winkler business or DCN business."

"Oh, well, it still sounds mysterious."

We agreed to meet at a café on Rue St. Honore near her hotel.

I caught the Metro at Odeon, changed trains at Chatelet and took the number one line to the Place de la Concorde stop. I came up across the street from the plaza. The traffic moved quickly and I found one of the few crosswalks. I looked up as I crossed the street. At the other end of the famous Champs-Elysees was the Arc de Triomphe. What a magnificent sight. Certainly reduces the importance of my problem.

My problem.

I walked up to the café. A few tables and chairs were piled up and chained together near the door. The owner no doubt figured outdoor seating was over for another year. Once inside, I heard Denise say my name. She was sitting at a small round table in the window. She stood up to greet me. She wore jeans, tight jeans, an off-white cable stitch sweater and tennis shoes.

"I'm having a late breakfast," she said. "How about you?"

"No, thanks. Café au lait, s'il vous plait," I said to the waiter.

Denise ordered an omelet and a Chardonnay. "My curiosity is killing me," she said. "What's the business you want to talk about?"

"Do you remember my brother, Tom? I told you about him at dinner."

"Of course."

"Well, it's about him, and I could use your help. By the way, do you know anything about football?"

"Are you kidding?" she said. "I grew up on season tickets to the Bears. The company has ten tickets last time I looked." Denise took a drink of wine. "So it's really not about the company or Harold?"

"No, not at all. In fact, there is some risk to it." Her face and eyes brightened at the suggestion.

"Do tell," she said, with a barely concealed smile.

I filled her in on the sordid details I'd left out earlier. She ate her omelet and listened.

"Geez," she said, shaking her head. "I thought my life was nuts, but you have some really strange friends."

"Tell me about it."

"Your brother seems awfully naïve, if you don't mind me saying so."

"I don't mind," I said, "because it's true."

"All right, how do I fit in?"

I explained what I wanted. It was a sketchy plan, at best. Of course, it was barely six hours old. It hadn't had enough time to marinate.

Denise finished her omelet and ordered coffee.

"Denise, I want to say this as clearly as possible. You will be in some danger if you do this."

"Is Clare's husband, what's his name again?"

I told her.

"Right. Is Rick Morgan really likely to kill your brother?"

"Yes. If not him, his gunslinger, Vanelli, would do it. If things get really ugly, the rest of us could get hurt, too."

"Frank, I like that you want me to be a part of this," she said. "So don't take this as a no because it's not." Denise hesitated.

"Why don't you just call the Paris cops? Les gendarmes. Wouldn't that be easier?"

It was the right question for a smart person to ask. "If I do that," I said, "here's what I think would happen. The cops would probably hold Morgan or Vanelli on something. Maybe the guns. No one's dead or hurt yet, so they wouldn't be held very long."

"They kidnapped your brother," Denise said. "What about that?"

"Maybe the cops believe Tommy, maybe they don't." I sipped my coffee. "In any case, the real problem is Clare. She gets wind we called the cops, she's gone and takes the money with her. Morgan'll never let Tommy alone. And he'll search for Clare until he finds her and the money. Nobody's safe. But if I can make the deal for the money, maybe everybody goes home."

"Well, I'm not sure about your rationale," Denise said. "Still... do you remember that day in your office when I explained why I chased around with the recently departed Mr. Donaldson? I feel the same way now. I want in on your scheme because I want to do some exciting things with the rest of my life. I hear your concern for my safety. I appreciate it, believe me. But you've offered me a very interesting escapade, to say the least, and I'm in. What's the first step?"

"We pay the bill," I said.

"Smart ass! I like smart asses, Frank, and I like you. So, really, what is the first step?"

"First, I call Clare Morgan."

There was a public phone in the back, near the kitchen. Leaning against the wall, out of the way of the waiters hustling back and forth, I dialed the number.

"Madame Harvey, s'il vous plait," I said to the operator at the Hotel de Saxe. Clare came on the line. When I suggested that we meet to talk details, she cautiously agreed. Maybe escaping to Eastern Europe wasn't as viable a plan as mine. Scary thought. I told her that a friend I trusted, a woman, was coming along to help. That, too, was okay. But Clare drew the line at meeting anywhere near the Right Bank.

"Still worried your husband will find you?"

"Of course, I am," she said in an irritated tone. "Why take chances now. You want to tell me what you have in mind?"

"Soon," I said. "You want to meet at the Eiffel Tower again?"

"Yes," she said, "same place as before."

I went back to the table. Denise had paid the bill and left a tip. "Well?"

"It's all set," I said. "We'll meet her in an hour over by the Eiffel Tower."

"Good. I've got a rental car. Shall we drive?"

"You drive in this town?" I said, astonished that any sane person would try it.

"Of course I do," she said, laughing. "It's part of the fun. Besides, my football gear's in the trunk."

I looked at her, and we laughed.

"Leave the thing parked. Have you been on the Metro yet?" I asked.

"Oui, Monsieur Marshall. C'est rapide et facile."

We left the cafe and walked down Rue Royale to the Concorde Metro stop. We rode the number eight train to École Militaire.

"Have you heard from your daughter or Harold?" I asked.

She told me that the stock transfer was complete and that she was legally in control of DCN Manufacturing. Harold volunteered to go with her to confront her stepsons with the unwelcome news.

"Will you keep them in the company?" I asked. "Assuming they play by your rules?"

"No." And that was all she said on the matter.

We climbed the stairs to the street. The air was cool and a few clouds wandered the sky, but they held no rain. We made our way along the dirt paths near the Eiffel Tower. The grass was quite green for so late in the year. I pointed to a bench in the trees and we sat down and waited for Clare.

"Tell me about Clare Morgan," Denise said. "Not more of your crazy stories, I want to know something about her as a woman."

I described her as best I could. I only knew the public side of her. "She's more 'femme fatale' than genuine woman, if you know what I mean."

Denise nodded her head.

"Of course, I misjudged her intelligence more than once. It seems like the smart woman surfaced in her obsessive need to get away from her husband."

"It sounds like she's spent most of her adult life trading on the sexy-woman façade," Denise said. "Perhaps the real person, the clever bright woman started to come out as she's gotten older, you know, less physically attractive?"

"She hasn't lost much in that department," I said, apparently a bit eagerly.

"Why, Mr. Marshall, do I detect a hint of lusty interest?"

"If you're asking am I attracted to Clare Morgan, the answer is yes. If you're asking if that attraction would push me to do anything to jeopardize my relationship with Ellen, the answer is no."

Denise leaned forward and put a hand on my arm. "Frank, you're in Paris. Clare's about to go to Prague, or some damn place, and you'll probably never see her again. Who's to know if you spend a couple of nights together?"

"I'm surprised that you would even ask a question like that," I said.

"I'm not advocating action, Frank. I'm just curious about your motives."

Across the way, two young mothers talked as they pushed strollers.

"To be honest, it isn't just Ellen."

Denise looked at me and squinted her eyes.

"I'm rapidly losing interest in people who have so little regard for other people. People who live their lives as if yesterday never existed, as if the damage they cause isn't real."

Denise looked over my shoulder and straightened up. I turned around and saw Clare Morgan walking toward us. She wore black stretch pants, low-heeled boots and the same navy warm-up jacket from the other day. I wondered if she wore anything under it this time. Her blond hair was loose. It moved as she walked.

Denise stood up. "Hello, Clare," she said. "I'm Denise Kirshner. I hear you're in trouble."

Clare held Denise's hand for a moment and said, "Yeah. I guess I am." Clare obviously had a positive first impression. I got no read off Denise about Clare.

We sat on the bench. The young mothers had taken over another bench. One baby slept in a stroller. The other had the undivided attention of both mothers.

Clare wasted no time. "What have you got in mind?" she asked me. Before I could answer, she asked, "Who gets the money?"

"I'd rather you listen to the whole thing. Then make up your mind."

"That means my husband gets the money, doesn't it?" she said, fatalistically.

Before I could say anything, Denise said, "Hear him out, okay? If you don't like, so be it. But the guy's trying to help you. How about it?"

"What about you?" Clare asked Denise. "Why are you here?"

"Because Frank asked me to be here and I said yes."

Clare looked hard at Denise. "Okay," she said. "I'm listening."

"Your husband's got Tommy." No point pulling punches.

"What do you mean he's got Tommy?" she asked, stunned. "You mean kidnapped?"

"That's it."

"Is he all right? Have you seen him? Talked to him?" The questions came out fast. Clare was so surprised that she lost her customary cool.

"I talked with him for a second last night," I said. "Morgan put him on the phone long enough to know he's okay."

"What does he want?" she asked more deliberately. She likely knew the answer.

"You and the money."

"Is there an 'or else' attached to that?"

"You run off with the money and Morgan has Vanelli kill Tommy. Then they come for you and the money."

Clare leaned forward, elbows on her knees, head in her hands. I caught Denise watching Clare carefully, measuring her.

"He will kill Tommy," Clare said, softly. She raised her head and looked at me.

"Ricky'll have Tommy murdered as a warning to me. No matter how long it takes, he'll come for me." She shook her head. "Shit. He gets me one way or the other. The money, too."

"There might be another way," I said. "But I have to know something. Would he kill Tommy if he gets what he wants?"

Clare shrugged. "There'd be no point. He'll scare Tommy bad enough and he'll keep me under lock and key. Ricky's not into murder if there's no gain."

"All right, then," I said. "See what you think of this."

Clare shifted herself around on the bench.

"First, Morgan gets the money."

Clare shook her head in a defiant way that said, "shove it" more than "I don't like it." Denise reached out and gently touched her arm. Denise catches on fast and she has an instinct for people.

"He has to get the money, Clare," I said. It's the only leverage we got. Look, I want to save Tommy's ass, you want to get permanently away from your husband. The money's the only thing we've got to trade."

"That's easy for you to say, for crissake," Clare said. "At least you've got a job in that tight-assed law firm of yours. What am I supposed to do? Live off my rapidly fading good looks?" She got off the bench and walked a few feet up the path and stood there looking up at the tower.

Denise tapped my shoulder and pointed at Clare. She whispered, "Go on."

"How much of the million is left?" I asked.

"About 850 or 900 thousand," she answered, still staring at the tower. "I haven't spent that much." Suddenly, she walked back towards us, put her hands on her hips and said, "What makes you think my husband's going to take the money and go home? Do you seriously think he'd leave me alone and let Tom off the hook?" Scared or not, she asked hard questions. This was no time for bullshit answers.

"I don't know," I said. "I haven't figured that out yet."

"Wonderful. You have no idea how big Rick's ego is. You talk like he's rational."

"Clare, I'll find a way. If Morgan'll take a trade, and I'm going to give him one. If I don't show up with you and the money, Tommy's dead. One way or the other, we have to play this out. I'll make it up as I go."

Clare stood there, shaking her head. "That's some plan you got there."

"Look, Clare, I think he'd settle for the money and forget about you if... if he was convinced that you wanted to be alone, not with any man, especially not with Tommy."

"How will you manage that?" she asked, sarcastically.

"That's where I come in," Denise said. Instincts and a sense of timing.

"You?"

"Uh, huh, me."

"I'm going to tell your husband that Denise will help you get set up on your own. You don't want Rick's money and you don't want Tom. Denise will come with us. It will be more convincing that way."

A group of fifty or so Japanese tourists walked by towards the Eiffel Tower. A guide, holding a huge map, talked steadily, loudly as she walked next to the others. She looked to be half their age. She had a difficult time keeping up.

"Let's suppose," Clare said, "for some stupid fucking reason, that my husband buys your scenario. Like I said before, what the hell am I supposed to live on?"

"How about a job?" It was Denise. Clare shot her a look.

"A job?" Clare said. "You mean work?"

"That's exactly what I mean."

"It's not my style," Clare said, petulantly.

If Denise was annoyed, she didn't show it. I was annoyed.

"Look, you want out of your marriage," Denise said. "Isn't that right?" Clare nodded. If Frank can get your husband to leave you alone, I'll take care of the rest."

Clare waited for an explanation.

"I run a company in Chicago," Denise said. "It's a fairly large manufacturing business. You've got a job, if you want it. It won't be a make-work job either. It'll be a real job in the office and you'll start at the bottom. You'll have to work your way up just like everybody else, but I'll pay you a fair wage and give you decent benefits. I assume you don't have much more than clothes right now. I own an apartment building an easy bus ride from the office. I'll give you a furnished one-bedroom—rent-free—for one year while you get on your feet. After that, you're on your own. It's a fresh start. What do you say?"

Clare looked stunned, again, only this time she had tears in the corners of her eyes. "I don't know what to say. No one's ever said anything like that to me." Clare sat down on the bench between us. "Why would you want to help me? You don't even know me." The tears ran down her cheeks now. She pulled a tissue from her jacket pocket.

"I know more about you than you think," Denise said. Clare looked at me. "Frank told me about you, sure, but I know your life because I lived it." Clare looked at Denise again. "Oh, my husband didn't slap me around, not physically anyway, but his disrespect left its mark. I married too young. I spent a lot of his money. I had plenty of lovers. I thought the humiliation didn't matter. It did. One day I discovered I had no self-respect. But I was lucky. The company was my life jacket. Without it, well, I don't know. I was lucky."

Clare sat, but didn't say a word.

"I want to help you because I can. That may not seem like much of a reason to some people, but it means a lot to me."

Denise put her hand out to Clare. "You can't hide for the rest of your life. It's time to stand up for you. You're more than just a body, Clare. It's been there all along but you're still figuring it out. Do you want to live a Hollywood fantasy gone sour with the Rick Morgans of the world, or do you want a chance at a real life? A life where you are the one who counts."

"Could it really work?" Clare asked.

"I think it's got a chance," I said, trying to be honest. "If you being alone doesn't hurt Morgan's ego as much as running off with another man, we've got a good chance."

"What about Tommy?"

"Let me worry about him," I said. "If you go with Denise, Morgan gains nothing by hurting Tommy. This might be the best way to save his life."

"Can you make it work?" she asked me again.

"It's our best shot," I said. But I didn't answer her question.

Denise put her arms around Clare and gave her a hug. Clare began to sob openly. The more painful the crying, the more she allowed herself to be held by Denise. I left the two them alone and walked to the food stand at the base of the tower and bought three small bottles of Evian. I took my time.

We sat on the bench for a while. "Well, Clare," Denise said, "what do you think? You game to try it?"

Clare rubbed her puffy eyes. "I guess so. What choice do I have?"

"Denise, I want you to move to Clare's hotel. I don't want you to leave her side until this is over. And bring your car."

"Consider it done."

"Is that okay with you, Clare?" Denise asked.

Clare nodded and told her how to find the hotel.

"I'll call Morgan and set up the meet. A public place. Enough to keep us safe."

Denise asked Clare to go with her to pack, but Clare refused because it was only a few blocks from her husband's hotel. "I'll get to your hotel as quickly as I can," Denise assured her.

The three of us walked back up the Champ de Mars. Denise went underground at the École Militaire Metro stop. I walked with Clare around the school to catch the number 4 train back to my hotel.

"We'll make this work, Clare," I said. I put my arms around her. She nestled into my body with the innocence of a lost child. "I'll call as soon as it's set."

"We're ready on this end," I said to Rick Morgan. "Is my brother all right?"

"You got the broad and the money?" he asked, ignoring my question.

"Yes," I said. I lied. "What about Tom?"

"The professor's in fine shape. I guarantee it."

"Let's get it done, then."

Morgan wanted the meeting in his hotel room.

"Not a chance," I said. "Some place we can all feel safe. Some place public."

"You don't have much choice if you want to see your brother again."

"Neither do you."

Morgan hesitated. "What've you got in mind?"

"Eiffel Tower, at dawn," I said. "You heard of it?"

"Fuck you, asshole. Make sure you got the broad and the money." He slammed the receiver down.

I called the Saxe Hotel. Denise had checked in and she picked up the phone on the first ring. I told her everything was ready.

"I'm in the room next to Clare," she said. "I'll tell her."

"Only a few hours more and it should be all over," I said. "You did a good job convincing Clare to take the risk and give up the money."

"I know," she said, "now you convince Morgan to do the same with Clare."

CHAPTER 25

My watch read 4:10. Why I thought I would sleep is beyond me. I clicked off the alarm and switched on the lamp next to the bed. My eyes stung from being tired and from the sudden burst of light. I propped the pillows up behind my head.

I could make this work. Clare had done her part, despite being scared. Her life changed forever the day she took the money and ran, but at least now she'd have a chance at a decent life. With Denise's help. Tommy wouldn't have any choice but to go along if he wanted to live. Morgan was the wild card. If he took the money and called it even, the plan works. If he didn't...

I was annoyed as hell that I had to trust Morgan to do what was in his best interest. I had to trust a two-bit tough guy more than my brother. Sad. But Morgan's decision was cleaner, without the baggage that Tommy carried all the time. If Morgan decided to forget about Clare and Tommy, that'd be that. But Tommy would always have a tornado of conflicting feelings whirling around him.

Maybe if I had a gun. Vanelli had one, so did Morgan for all I knew. "What the fuck's the point?" I said out loud. "I pull a gun, I get shot. Lotta good that'll do." No, a gun wouldn't make this work.

I bet Ellen was sitting in bed reading one of those trashy novels she liked so much. I'd have liked to be next to her dozing off, waiting for her to cuddle up behind me until we drifted off to sleep or made love. Either one would've felt nice right then.

Right then? Right then, I had to concentrate on what was ahead.

I threw back the covers as if I were mad at them. The adrenalin pumped hard. I sat up and pulled back the drapes. I was getting even more damned irritated at starting my days this way. It was still dark, but the wet streets reflected light from the street lamps. I turned on the shower and let the water warm up. I got in and gradually moved the lever hotter and hotter. I stood there with the water beating down on my head. It helped.

This was one of those days when confidence could make the difference. So I shaved. Hell, if I'd had a power outfit—black suit, white shirt, tie—I'd have worn it. I settled for wrinkled khakis, a black turtleneck, a heavy cotton crew-neck and running shoes.

The dining room was closed and the night clerk was nodding off behind the desk. His glasses had slipped down his nose.

I walked down the street towards the Odeon Metro stop. A light mist drifted in the air. I couldn't see it, not even in the streetlights, but I could feel it. A small shop with a carryout window on the sidewalk was open. It was empty except for the counter man who sat on a stool, arms folded, looking for something to do. I bought a large coffee to go. It was hot, black and tasted like cardboard. But the heat felt good going down.

I took the number 4 line to the Segur stop. Only one other person rode in my car. He sat at the far end, hunched over, asleep or drunk or both. It was still dark when I got to the Hotel

Saxe. No one was at the desk, so I turned left and went up the stairs. Room 3-A was halfway down the hall. I knocked softly.

Denise opened the door. "Come on in," she said. She wore the same jeans and tennis shoes as yesterday. Her navy sweatshirt said "Mackinac Island" on the front.

"You've been to the island?" I asked before saying hello.

"Love it," she said. "Go there all the time."

"Me, too. Where's Clare?"

Denise pointed to the bathroom.

"You two get any sleep?"

Denise shook her head. "Not really. We spent most of the night talking. Getting to know each other." Denise sat on the bed. I sat on a bench next to the window. "I like her, Frank. I don't like some of the nasty things she's done, and I told her so, but she's had a rough time. Not just with Morgan. Did you know that Morgan's her second husband?"

I shook my head.

"Uh, huh. The first one drank too much, blew his head off with a shotgun and left a note blaming her. He also left a stack of bills and she had no job. Rick and his money were pretty seductive, let me tell you." Denise leaned forward, elbows on her knees. "Clare's funny, you know, sort of odd. She's scared about today, but she's smart enough to know that this is her best chance to be rid of Morgan. She doesn't like the idea of working for a living, of course, but she's going for it anyway."

"Assuming this works," I said.

Denise shrugged.

There was a knock at the door. "You expecting anyone?" I asked.

"Room service with coffee," Denise said. She opened the door and took a tray from a woman in her fifties who looked too sleepy to be happy about the job. Denise put down the tray and I poured.

Clare came out of the bathroom wearing jeans, a red and white striped sweater and tennis shoes. I felt overdressed.

"Good morning, Frank."

"How are you doing?"

"Okay, I guess. " She folded her arms across her chest and sat next to Denise on the bed. "I don't know what's going to happen, but I'll feel better when it's over."

The coffee was much better than my last cup. I went over the details of what I wanted them to do. I opened the window and looked east. No light in the sky, but it was getting late.

"Where's you car?" I asked Denise.

"Couple of blocks over," she said. "Just take a minute to get there."

"Where's the money, Clare?" I tried to sound like all I wanted was a map of the city.

She handed me a leather case slightly larger than a carton of cigarettes. I opened it and pulled out one pack of bills with a red rubber band around it. One thousand dollar bills.

"Looks familiar," I said.

Clare laughed. "That seems like a long time ago. How much did I offer you?"

"Two hundred thousand."

"That much," she said, laughing again.

I put the pack of bills back in the case and gave it to Clare. I poured each of us more coffee. I added some hot milk to mine this time.

"How much is left?"

"To be exact, $877,000," she said. "And I'm keeping two thousand as folding money whether you like it or not, Frank."

I didn't say a word.

A smile crept across Clare's face.

"What is it?" Denise asked, smiling, too.

"Oh, Tommy and I had a lot of fun spending Ricky's money," Clare said. "Restaurants, hotels, always the best. I felt so free, like I'd flown away and he could never find me. Boy, was that dumb." She shook her head and the tears came. Denise put her arms around Clare and hugged her. Clare tried to say something, but she buried her head in Denise's shoulder instead. Denise held her, I drank coffee and no one said a word.

After a few minutes, Clare was sitting up drying her eyes and sipping coffee. I looked at my watch. "It's getting late."

"Before we go," Clare said. "I'd like to say something. Since yesterday, I've been thinking about what you two are doing for me. Frank, I know you're trying to save Tom, but you're also doing something for me. Even the idea of working doesn't sound so bad, after the initial shock, anyway."

Denise smiled.

"I always thought the world owed me a living, and look where it got me?" She shook her head. "Taking care of myself sounds scary, if you want the truth. I have no idea how to do that."

Denise started to talk, but Clare waved her off.

"I know what you're going to say, and I accept your help, I really do. Anyway, whatever happens, thank you. I've never felt more cared about than I do right now." She gave Denise a hug.

"It's time," I said.

CHAPTER 26

The desk in the lobby was still without a night clerk. We went outside and down the street. The mist had turned into drizzle and I tugged my collar up around my neck. Denise's blue Peugeot sedan was parked near a driveway, two blocks away. She unlocked the doors and we climbed in, Clare in the front, me in the back. Denise started the motor and switched on the wipers. We drove around the military school, up Avenue de la Bourbonnais, turned left onto a side street and stopped in the parking lot at the base of the Eiffel Tower. Three other cars sat in the lot. The nearest one, an old Citron 2CV, had a flat tire. During the day, cars filled the lot and tour busses lined the street.

Every inch of the tower was covered with lights. The area around the tower was also very bright, but the lights cast eerie shadows off the trees, the food stand and the cars in the lot. Behind the trees, to the east, I could see the pale light of sunrise in the clouds.

I leaned forward with my arms resting on the seat backs. "Okay, you ready?"

They nodded.

"Stay here until I signal you. Then out of the car and walk right up to us. I want Morgan to see both of you, especially Denise. Remember, if gunplay starts, I'll distract them somehow. Run for the car. Get the hell out of here and don't come back."

"I don't see Rick anywhere," Clare said.

"Neither do I," I said. "But I doubt that he's hiding in the bushes in the rain."

"He'll come by car." Clare said confidently.

"Well, here we go."

I got out of the car and walked to the large, round open area covered with small pebbles, underneath the middle of the tower. I didn't see anyone, not even street people trying to hide from the drizzle. A few cars sped by on the Quai Brenly, 100 yards away. I pulled my collar tighter against the wet, pushed my hands into the jacket pockets and waited.

The light in the east was clear and distinct, but the western sky was still full dark when I heard a car pull into the lot across the open area from Denise's car. No headlights or running lights. The driver's door opened and the dome light outlined three people. Tony Vanelli got out from behind the wheel. He looked at me, stuck his head back in the car and said something. The passenger door opened and out came Rick Morgan. He closed the door and walked towards me. He looked around. Vanelli stayed at the car, resting his arms on the open door. My heart was pounding, the noise of the pebbles crunching under Morgan's feet seemed deafening. He had on a long raincoat, but his hands were not in the pockets. He wore gloves. Ten feet away from me, he stopped.

"Marshall," he said.

I didn't say anything.

"Where's Clare and the money?"

"Where's Tommy?" Point, counter-point.

"I told you to bring my wife and the money." He sounded edgy, like I'd welched on the deal. I didn't want to raise the stakes.

"In the car," I said, nodding towards Denise's Peugeot. He looked over.

Morgan raised his left arm like he was hailing a cab on Michigan Avenue. Vanelli turned and opened the rear door. Out stepped Tommy. Vanelli pushed Tommy in front of him and the two men walked slowly towards us. When they got close enough, Vanelli grabbed Tommy's shoulder and they both stopped. I caught a glimpse of Vanelli's holster under his blue windbreaker.

Tommy looked awful. His face was covered with stubble, his hair was matted and he had a cut at the corner of his mouth. He stood next to Vanelli, head down, staring at the pebbles under his feet.

"You all right, Tommy?" I asked. He didn't say anything, but his head moved slowly up and down.

"The professor's fine," Morgan said. "Tony hasn't laid a glove on him since the first time." That would be the cut lip.

I waved at Denise's car. The doors opened and the two women got out and came towards us. They stopped across from Tommy and Vanelli and the six of us formed a circle under the Eiffel Tower.

"Who's the broad?" Morgan asked suspiciously.

Before I could answer, Denise said, "I'm Denise Kirshner, if that's any business of yours."

Morgan laughed. "Christ. Everybody's a comic. What are you, her babysitter?"

"Friend," Denise said, "I'm her friend. She doesn't need a babysitter."

"All right, friend," Morgan said, dragging out the word "friend" sarcastically. He looked over at me. "What's she doing here? What the fuck's she doing here?"

Denise fielded that question, too. "I'm here because Clare wants me here. And if you have another question for me, ask me."

Morgan shook his head. "For crissake, Tony. Nobody talks to me that way back home." He shook his head again and said to all of us, "Let's do the business we came here to do and get the fuck outta here. Where's the money?"

"A couple of things have changed," I said.

Morgan stiffened and shot a look at Vanelli. Tony moved both hands to his hips, which pushed the sides of his jacket back so everyone could see his gun. A .45 automatic.

"We had a deal, smart guy."

"We still do," I said quickly, trying to prevent either of them from pulling a gun. "You'll get the money. We'll trade for Tom Marshall." Tommy didn't react at the mention of his name. I wasn't sure he knew where he was, let alone what was happening.

"The deal was Marshall for the money and my wife," Morgan said. "This is the second time you've lied to me, punk."

"This is different, Rick!" It was Clare. She took all of us by surprise. Even Tommy reacted. His head came off his chest and he stared at her. Clare pulled the leather case from an inside coat pocket.

"Here," she said, handing the case to Morgan. "Here's the money. Most of it anyway. I don't want it anymore."

Morgan took the case. He opened it and looked inside. "How much?"

"I only spent a hundred thousand, or so," she said. "The rest of it's there."

Morgan's eyes moved around the circle. They stopped on me. I knew what he was thinking. "I can take this," he held up the case, "and my wife and walk away. You can't stop me."

"That's right," I said. I raised my right hand as if I were taking an oath. With the left hand, I slowly unzipped my jacket. Vanelli turned my way. "Don't get nervous, Tony," I said. I pulled open the sides of my jacket. "No gun. You want to walk away now, do it." I was bluffing. My instincts said Morgan was too uncertain to do that. "But listen to Clare, first. What have you got to lose?"

Morgan shuffled his feet in the stones. So far, so good. "All right, Clare," he said, "you got two minutes."

Clare turned towards her husband said, "I don't want to be married anymore, Ricky. I want out. I want a divorce."

If Morgan had a reaction, it didn't show. Tommy, on the other hand, smiled.

"Clare?" Tommy said, almost whispering. Denise heard him. So did I. Clare didn't.

"I should have told you, Rick," Clare said. "I should have told you what I wanted, but I knew you would never let me go. So I took the money and ran." She took a step towards him. "Ricky, all I want is to go away, to be by myself. I... I have to do this."

"Clare?" It was Tommy again, but this time everyone heard him. "Honey, let's get out of here. Let's go away."

"What do you take me for," Morgan said, angrily, " a pussy-chump? Is that what I am to you?" He glared at Tommy, then at Clare. "I gotta stand here and listen to this shit?" He jabbed his finger in the air and pointed at Clare. "You're not going anywhere with this asshole. Is that clear?"

Vanelli never took his eyes off me. I was the only threat, the only one he wasn't sure about, the only one who might try something.

"Rick!" Clare said, sharply. "Damnit, Ricky, listen to me. For once in your life, listen to me. I don't want him. Do you hear me? I don't want him. I don't want any man. I just want to go away... alone." Morgan heard the words, but they didn't register. The blank stare on his face said that he didn't get it.

Tommy interrupted again. "Clare! What do you mean? You don't want me?" Tommy tried to move forward but Tony caught him by the hair and yanked backwards. "Ahhh," Tommy screamed. He reached up, but Vanelli pulled back hard and sat Tommy on the ground.

"Tony," I said. "Take it easy."

Tommy tried to push himself off the stones, but Vanelli put the palm of his hand on the top of Tommy's head and pressed down.

"Sit, asshole," Vanelli said. "Stay there."

"I never wanted him, Rick," Clare said. "He was somebody to help, that's all. I used him. I used him, too." She pointed at me.

"I figured the brothers would keep you busy long enough for me to get away."

"You telling me you fucked this guy for nothing? Is that what you're telling me?"

"It goes with the territory," she said. It came out like ice. "I did what I had to do. You ought to understand that."

I couldn't tell what Morgan was thinking. I said nothing. Clare was doing all right by herself.

"Clare, what are you saying? You love me, you know you do." Tommy was pleading with her. He sat on the stones, his legs out in front of him, with his arms stretched out towards her. "Tell him," he said, nodding at Morgan, "tell him you love me."

"Grow up, Tom," she said. "People come together, people go apart. That's just the way it is."

"Clare, why are you saying that? What are you doing?" Tommy started to laugh. "Oh, I get it. I'll play along." He had that over eager tone in his voice.

"This isn't a game, Tom," she said. It came out more irritated than angry.

Tommy began to sob openly, his chest heaving with each gasp for air.

Morgan stared at Tommy, disgusted. "You limp-dick piece of shit," he said. He looked at Clare. "You fucked this asshole? This is why I got pissed off?"

Tommy saw Morgan staring at him. "What are you looking at me for? It... it was all her fault," he said, pointing at Clare. "She started this. She's the one." He had turned ugly, mean. It happened that fast.

"Nobody dances alone, asshole," Morgan said.

"You planned this," Tommy hissed at Clare. "You're going to get me killed."

Even if what Tommy said was true, it was the wrong thing to say and we all knew it.

Crack! Vanelli caught Tommy on the side of the head with the back of his hand. "Ahh," Tommy yelled, and rolled into a heap on the ground holding his head. Vanelli reached down for him.

"He's not worth killing," I said. "Let him go. You kill him, you'll have to kill all of us."

Tommy got up on his knees, rubbing the side of his head.

"All Clare wants is to go away," I said.

"I'm going to help her," Denise chimed in, sensing the right time to talk.

"Just what are you going to do for her?" Morgan asked. He didn't sound annoyed or angry. More like confused.

"I'll set her up," Denise said. "A place to live, a job."

"A job?" Morgan said, astonished. "She's gonna work?"

"Yes, I am," Clare answered, nodding her head.

"Let Tommy go." I repeated. "He's not worth killing. Take the money and forget about him. Give Clare what she wants."

Morgan looked over at Vanelli and shook his head. That was it. Tommy was a dead man. But Tony zipped up his jacket and stuffed his hands into the pockets.

"Denise," I said, clearly but softly, "take Clare and get out of here." Clare looked at me, then at her husband. Morgan never looked at her, but he said, "Go on." Denise took Clare's arm and the two women turned and walked quickly to the car.

I kept my eyes on Morgan and Vanelli. Tommy was still on his knees. I heard the Peugeot's motor snap to life and the gears mesh as Denise drove away.

The two men stood over Tommy. "Tony," Morgan said. Vanelli turned on his heels and started for the car. Morgan put his hands in the pockets of his coat and headed for the car. He glanced over his shoulder at me, but he kept walking. They got into the car and drove away. The sky was full light now, but there would be no sun. Traffic had picked up on the Quai Brenly.

Tommy was still on his knees, crying softly.

"What am I going to do?" he said, gasping for air. "She's gone, Frank. You gotta help me get her back."

"Go back to the States, Tommy. I'm through helping you. That's your job from now on."

He gasped again. "What'll I do, Frank?"

"I don't know, Tommy. I don't want to know."

I was wet to the skin and suddenly very cold. I walked away and left Tommy Marshall to himself.

CHAPTER 27

The shower was hot. I stood there for a long time trying to force the chill out of my skin. Finally, I shut the water off and grabbed a towel.

The room was warm and moist from the shower and the window was fogged. I still felt cold. I shaved, brushed my hair, put on a fresh pair of khakis, my last, a white turtleneck and a navy sweatshirt with nothing written on the front. I stuffed clothes into my bags. I put on a pair of black penny loafers and kept the blazer as a jacket. I was aware of details, the mundane details of life, of pants, of shoes, of packing. I wanted to pay more attention to unimportant things.

I picked up the phone. It was almost four in the morning in Chicago. I dialed the code and the number. The line opened on the other end. I heard muffled noises and then a very groggy, "Hello?"

"Ellen. Hi," I said. "It's me."

She woke up fast. "Frank! Oh, my god, Frank! You all right?"

"Yes. I'm all right."

"You startled me."

"I'm sorry. I didn't mean to frighten you, but I don't have much time."

"Sure you're okay?" she asked again.

"Yeah. I'm coming home. They got me on the last seat on the one o'clock to O'Hare. In the smoking section. Can you believe that?"

"What happened to Tommy?"

"You were right," I said. "He wasn't worth it. They're all messy people, Ellen."

"I'm sorry, Frank. Life is a mess sometimes. Things aren't always neat and tidy." I looked at my neatly packed bags, wet clothes here, dirty clothes there, all zipped up and ready to go.

"I know, but all of them...even Tommy. They're reckless people, Ellen."

"What about Tommy?" she asked again.

"He's alive," I said. "That's as good as it gets." I knew that would make no sense to Ellen, but I didn't have the energy for more. "I'll tell you all about it when I get home. I'm too tired. That okay?"

"Sure," she said. "I'll meet you at the airport."

"I'd like that. I'd like to feel your arms around me, too."

"That can be arranged," she said softly.

"I've missed you, Frank. I didn't like the way we left things."

"I didn't like it either, Ellen. If I hadn't been so caught up in Tommy's world, I might have heard what you were trying to tell me. I'm the one who put us in this uncomfortable place."

"Let's sort that out when you get home," she said. "We have a good track record at sorting things out. We can do it again."

"I'd like to spend Thanksgiving weekend with your family, if that's still on the agenda?"

"I talked to Mom and Dad yesterday," she said. "They're expecting us. They're also expecting snow. Maybe we can run over to Boyne and tune up the skis."

"Sounds like fun," I said. "See you in few hours."

I hung up the phone and checked again to see that everything was packed. I called the desk to have my bill ready and ordered a cab. I had an hour left and a couple of things to do.

I walked up the street and turned left at the Odeon Theatre onto Rue Racine. The drizzle had stopped sometime after I gotten back to the hotel, but steel gray clouds hung over the city. The white marble columns of the Odeon stood out in marked contrast to the heavy clouds, as if the theatre was ready to have its picture taken for a postcard. I'd walked by this building often during my stay in Paris, but it seemed more majestic now that life was returning to normal.

I walked to a small shop I'd passed as often as the theatre. Rigedon sold handmade dolls and marionettes. I'd always looked in the window when I went by. The shop was dark inside, with a black ceiling and walls. Several marionettes were more than five feet tall, with gangly arms and strings as thick as small ropes.

"Bonjour, Monseiur," a woman in her sixties said as I came through the door. She sat on a stool next to a display case. I ducked my head twice to avoid low hanging marionettes on my way to the counter.

"Bonjour, Madame," I said. "Parlez-vous anglais?" I didn't have the energy to concentrate on translating the language today.

"Oui, Monseiur," she said. I speak English a little."

I pointed to a row of small dolls in the window. "How much, s'il vous plait?"

She told me and I picked out one with a blue beanbag body and a richly detailed and painted ceramic head. Ellen would find a prominent place for it in her apartment. The shopkeeper wrapped the doll for the trip home and I paid by credit card.

I returned to the Balcons to check out. I waited for the cab in the lobby, sipping my last café au lait and watching the tourists arrive from the morning planes.

When my cab, a dingy red Citron sedan with three dented fenders and a smashed headlamp, arrived, the driver put the bags in the trunk, but I kept the wrapped doll in my lap. It was my only connection to Ellen and Chicago, and I wasn't about to let it go.

At Aeroport Charles de Gaulle, security was tight and all business, but in less than sixty minutes, we were airborne. I opened the *Herald Tribune* I'd bought in the airport and settled in for the ride home. The printed words of the newspaper pages merged into all that happened since Tommy first called that morning months before. I couldn't get Tommy off my mind, so I quit trying. I put the papers on the floor, pulled the lever on my seat and eased back with my eyes closed.

I'd thought I knew my brother, but I didn't really know him at all. He was a college professor, an ideal career to many people. He was tall, charming and attractive to women. He mixed work with an active social life. He lived well. That was the Dr. Thomas Marshall I knew, that most people knew.

But Thomas Marshall was, really, still Tommy. Inside that professional body beat the heart and soul of a thirteen year old. A sad, lonely man out of touch with the world around him and out of touch with himself. His world had no history and no consequences. Whatever Tommy wanted, Tommy believed he had a right to have. That's who my brother really was. When he went after Clare Morgan, the façade collapsed. He ruined his life, and he almost ruined mine.

And I'd thought that pushing Rick Morgan around would satisfy my need to get even. It hadn't. Ellen had been right about that. Confronting Morgan in Chicago, in Paris, proved nothing. My fame didn't even last the requisite fifteen minutes. Maybe Ellen could help me sort out why I needed to do that.

Morgan's tough guy tactics were more obvious than Clare's nasty self-indulgence, or Tommy's childish behavior, but either way, other people got caught in the crossfire. I didn't want to live my life with people like that. The price was too high, the people too reckless, the satisfaction too empty. I'd had enough of all of them, especially my brother. He would never change. Neither would Morgan. Clare had a chance, anyway, but we'd see.

I wanted to be home, home in Chicago. A long day at the office, a peaceful run in Lincoln Park, dinner with Ellen. Occasionally, in the past, I'd second-guessed myself about working for Winkler, Norton and Barger. Digging through files or into a client's background seemed slow and uninteresting. Now, I wasn't so sure. Was the alternative a world where Rick

Morgan made the rules and Tony Vanelli enforced them? A world of chaos that could seduce my brother... or me?

Tommy Marshall had called me because he needed help. But the help he really needed couldn't come from me. Tom had all the trappings of the successful adult, but he'd been drifting backward before he could vote. The slide got faster and more turbulent because life, ultimately, was not the movies. Tommy Marshall was reaching for something he couldn't have, something that didn't exist. And he still hasn't learned that yet.

ACKNOWLEDGMENTS

In the early days of this project, Jacque Shoppell and Frances Barger were the first to help.

Years later, it was Aaron Stander's Mystery Writing Workshop at the Interlochen Center for the Arts, and the writers around the table in the summer of 2012, which renewed my interest. If I had not gone to the workshop, I would not have dug up the yellowed, dog-eared sheets of paper and begun writing again. Fran hounded me to go to the workshop and harassed me to revise the manuscript afterwards. Bless her heart.

Heather Shaw edited the manuscript. She made it livelier, smoother, and more interesting. She made it a book and helped me to be a better writer in the process.

Peter Marabell grew up in metro Detroit, spending as much time as possible street-racing on Woodward Avenue in the late 1950s or visiting the Straits of Mackinac. With a Ph.D. in History and Politics, Peter spent most of his professional career on the faculty at Michigan State University. He is the author of *Frederick Libby and the American Peace Movement*. As freelance writer, Peter worked in several professional fields including, politics, the arts, and health care. *More Than a Body* is his first novel. In 2002, Peter moved permanently to northern Michigan with his spouse and business partner, Frances Barger, to live, write, and work at their two businesses on Mackinac Island. All things considered, he would rather obsess about American politics after a good five-mile run on the hills of the Mackinac Island.